TIPPING
THE
SCALES

TIPPING
THE
SCALES

DANIELLE DUCREST

Lafayette, LA, USA   2025

Other Works by Danielle Ducrest:

Steam & Stained Glass Numbers 0-10: Steampunk Adult Coloring Designs

Steam & Stained Glass Collection 2: Steampunk Adult Coloring Designs

ONE

A FIFTY-FOOT DRAGON wouldn't fit in the shallow water so close to land. That was why Cayna liked to be in her human form at the start of this trick. It was the only way to sneak up on beachgoers.

When she went for a swim, crabs and fish knew to stay far away. Humans didn't share that same instinct. She maneuvered around dozens of feet, keeping far enough away that she was sure none of them had spotted her. Her sensitive ears picked up snippets of human conversation just above the waterline. She had about twenty minutes of air left. Cayna dug her fingers into the sand to keep herself from floating up to the surface. She pulled herself along, inch by inch. She saw nothing but water, sand, and wading feet, some bare, some clad in sandals.

A small pair of feet waded toward her. Cayna let them get close. She smiled. It was time to let them all know she was here.

Her human fingers untied the laces of her bikini. She lifted her foot and curled her toes around the tiny pieces of fabric. Her feet widened as they transformed, skin becoming thick leather as her toes curled into clutching talons. She pushed away from the sand with fingers already bending into clawed toes. Her arms widened into forelegs. Her hind legs thickened. Her frame of vision widened.

She burst free from the water, snout and horns first.

A dark-skinned boy, no older than seven with floaties on both arms, gaped at her. She would have grinned if her snout had allowed it. A beat of the wings that appeared on her back sent her up, halfway out of the water, until she towered over the boy. She let more beats of her wings carry her up, up and up. The fifty-foot shadow of her fully transformed body fell across the water.

Screams, gasps of surprise and shouts met her. Hundreds of eyes turned to watch her. Human arms pointed. "Cayna! It's Cayna!"

Salt water dripped off her blue-green scales. She hovered in the sky and peered down the beach, which stretched on for miles. Beachgoers, umbrellas and towels formed a nearly unending line up and down the coast, from one island to the next one, just barely in sight.

Not everyone had noticed her yet. As she left the shocked boy behind and flew along the beach, more heads looked up.

She pointed her snout toward the clouds and released a burst of red flame hotter than the sun beating down. Her audience let out wolf-whistles, whoops and applause. She was, undoubtedly, the highlight of their day.

Moments like this were so enjoyable, a nice change from the rest of her time. She'd taken a break to go on a swim, and that had been fun on its own, but now, she basked in the freedom to be completely herself in full view of so many humans.

But even a moment like this wasn't free of obligation. The yachts floating three miles off the coast got a good view, too, as she lit the sky on fire. She'd flown closer to them earlier and had determined they weren't dangerous. They were probably just partiers enjoying international waters, but it didn't hurt to send a message, just in case the coast guard boat holding position half a mile from the coast wasn't enough.

That was probably enough showing off. Cayna banked to the side and descended toward an empty expanse of beach, halfway between the shoreline and the strip of hotels. She landed on all fours.

Kids came running from among the umbrellas, laughing and calling her name.

Cayna took the opportunity to shake herself free of water, splashing the kids. They squealed and laughed, delighted.

Their parents jogged up behind them and stopped to stare at the American Dragon up-close.

Cayna released her grip on her bikini and rolled onto her back and then onto her stomach, letting the sand rub against as many scales as possible. Her scales itched from her dip in the salt water, and the abrasive sand scratched that itch in such a satisfying way.

She pulled in her wings and tail as she rolled to avoid hitting anyone. The kids still dodged around her, screeching, until their parents finally remembered they were parents and pulled the kids to a safer distance. She rolled back onto her feet, shook off the sand and walked off on her four legs. She left the bikini behind. She'd return for it in a moment.

"Bye, Cayna!" the kids called after her.

She wandered toward several seven-foot-tall mounds forming a broken barrier between the hotels and the ocean. The parents stopped their kids from following as she stepped carefully over a dune.

She found her backpack right where she'd left it, in the little valley among the dunes. That was all the privacy she was going to bother to find. She let herself shift. The space in the valley was tight one moment and then more than big enough the next. She shifted from dragon to human and back every day. The human form had long since become a second skin, but she never failed to notice the sheer size difference between the two forms.

Hotel guests in upstairs rooms could have seen her transformation, but Cayna didn't really care if someone saw her naked human form. Even after a century of bowing to American prudishness, their sentiments hadn't really rubbed off on her. It was amusing, really, how much they didn't seem to mind looking at her naked dragon form but got so angry and flustered if she tried to go without clothes in her human form.

She brushed off the sand coating nearly every inch of skin, which didn't feel as pleasant on human skin as it had on her scales. She reached into her backpack for a towel and her clothes. She dressed in the underwear, shorts and T-shirt she'd been wearing when she arrived on the beach two hours ago.

Her hearing was sharp enough to pick up the footsteps kicking their way over a mound of sand. A white man with messy brown hair appeared on the crest of the dune. He wore swim trunks and no shirt. His arms, normally pale, had turned red along with his chest and shoulders. She had a feeling he would be suffering tomorrow from a bad sunburn.

His hand covered his eyes. "Is it okay to look?"

"Go ahead," she said, amused. "It's Ray Boyer, isn't it?" She'd only ever seen him in suits under bright studio lights.

"Yep, that's me. It's good to see you again." He dropped his hand. "You wouldn't happen to have any sunscreen, would you? I've run out and I think I need to put some on again. I'll give it back next week."

She shook her head in disbelief as she pulled the bottle out of her backpack. She tossed it to him, then pulled out a pair of sandals and slid them on.

"Thanks." He opened the cap and frowned at the foil seal. "This bottle hasn't been opened."

"I don't need it." She never got sunburned. She had naturally bronzed skin and dark hair so she hardly needed to tan, but she'd known dragons with lighter skin in their human forms, and they didn't burn in the sun, either.

"So why carry it?"

She strung her backpack over her shoulder. "One of you is always getting sunburned. And then my protective instincts kick in." "Instincts" wasn't the right term, but it was as good a word as any. "You're a bit far from Jersey."

"Nah, they've got planes for that nowadays. You may have heard of them."

"Yes. Noisy things. The pilots never like it when I do loops around them."

"Er …" This, finally, made him pause. "You don't come close enough to, uh, scratch the metal or anything, do you?"

She smirked. "Of course not. That would be dangerous for everyone on the plane, and I'm here to protect, not to harm."

"Right. Um. Well, I'm here because I'm on vacation with my wife and our kids. It's spring break for them." He waved vaguely back toward the beach. "I saw you head over here and thought I'd just come over and say hi."

"And steal my sunscreen?"

He shrugged. "Maybe I'll sell it on eBay. Make some money," he said lightly. "No, I actually spotted you when you went into the water earlier. You were underwater for a while. Just how long can dragons hold their breath, anyway?"

"Ask me next week. I'll see you then, Mr. Boyer."

"See you in the studio," said Ray.

She walked along the beach, passing each hotel until she reached the one she'd liked the look of from the air.

Some people she strolled past on the beach recognized her and called after her, thanking her for the show. Most of the crowd paid her no mind. A dragon not in dragon form was never as interesting. She'd noticed that many times before, and today was no exception.

The hotel lobby was human-sized, just like all buildings. Cayna had a theory that builders never took dragon-sized dimensions into consideration. There was only one dragon in the country, so why would they bother making it easy for a dragon in dragon form to enter a building? She was lucky she had a human form to fall back on. Her human hand could pull open a door with ease. Her human form could step through it.

In the lobby, puddles shaped like human footprints formed tracks from the doors to the elevator. Cayna glanced down at them as she walked up to the counter.

The woman behind the counter gave her a distracted smile as she scanned Cayna's face. It was an expression Cayna saw often. She could take a guess what was going on in this woman's mind: She knew she'd seen Cayna before, she just couldn't place it, not yet.

Cayna made it easier by handing over her government-issued credit card and federal photo ID — the custom one with two very distinct headshots. "I'd like a room for one night, please, as high up as you have available. I believe you have windows that open."

The woman's eyes widened. "Of course, Ms. Maren."

"Mrs."

Her eyebrows dipped in confusion. "Oh, I'm sorry. Mrs. Maren."

Cayna felt confused, too. Why had she corrected the woman? Cayna hadn't thought about her marriage in a long time. It was likely no human alive remembered that she wasn't single. When *was* the last time she'd thought about her nest-mate? And why had she thought about him now, in the middle of a beach hotel lobby?

She was still troubled as she took the keys and followed the woman's directions to her room.

A shower took care of the salt and sand still on her skin and in her hair. Later, she climbed into the king-sized bed that was too big for her human frame but too small for her dragon form – all hotel beds were. She did her best to relax in her human form, but sleeping with sheets against skin was never as comfortable as scales on rocks.

In her dreams, claws raked down her scales. Someone's wings wrapped around her and held fast. She nipped his leg in response, but playfully, without tearing muscle. Hot breath smothered the air in a cavern. They lay on a floor of woven sticks and leaves, both coarse and soft in ways that hotel mattresses could have never hoped to match.

She woke late in the night. She stared at the blinking numbers of the desktop alarm clock. The hotel blankets were too smooth. Her skin crawled with the wrongness of being here. She'd slept in beds for almost a century. She'd thought she'd long since adjusted to it. So why would she dream of things she hadn't experienced in a hundred years?

The sheets shredded with a loud ripping sound as she threw them off of her. She held up her hand and realized it had turned into a scaly paw. She didn't bother turning it back to human. She used her other hand, still in human form, to throw her things into her backpack. She could see in the dark just fine.

She crossed the room to the window and climbed up onto the sill. The metal edges of the window frame dug into the pads of her human feet. She lifted one ankle behind her and draped the backpack straps over it.

She jumped and changed. Her ankle expanded as her leg transformed to a dragon's hind leg. The backpack straps fit like an ankle bracelet on her dragon-form leg.

Not many people on land were awake to witness the blue-green-scaled dragon take to the skies. But the passengers and pilots on the commercial flight she came across got a great view. It was climbing the sky outside the Miami airport. The plane was mostly dark except for a few caution lights on the fuselage. As she approached, shades rose as passengers crowded around the windows for a view of her. The frames of every window flared to life, LED lights pointed outwards, illuminating her like spotlights on a stage. Some airlines in the U.S. installed the special lights in every model of plane they built. Cayna had such a reputation for "playing" with commercial flights that the airlines had deemed the investment worth it.

Cayna circled the plane two more times, giving them the show they wanted, before soaring away.

She headed north over central Florida, then headed west across the Panhandle. She continued across the country, passing over the southern states and the southwestern states. The black splotches of lakes, channels and swamps were landmarks she'd long since memorized, easily recognizable among home-security lights and streetlights marking highways. She'd even driven down some of those roadways and walked inside many of those cities.

It took hours to reach the Pacific coast, but she wasn't traveling at her top speed. She left Florida behind in the middle of the night, and she arrived in the middle of the night in California. She thought about finding a spot on a slope and sprawling on the grass. But she began to flag while Sacramento stretched out below her and the mountains were too many miles away. Instead, she checked into another hotel, called the Miami hotel to tell them she'd checked out, and slept another twelve hours in a bed that felt as uncomfortable as the last. But at least, this time, she was too tired to dream.

The next day, she headed up north to Washington, then went east at a slower pace. She patrolled, watching every city she passed over, and as usual, found nothing at all.

She stopped again in Minnesota, found a hotel, then set off again after resting.

She did a full circuit of the country. It was her usual patrol. She watched the skies for enemies. She scanned the ground for dangers she could help with. She found none for her particular talents, so all was well.

Once upon a time, Cayna had done flybys along the border, but current United States relations with Canada and Mexico prevented her from doing so. She had to settle for patrolling close to but not directly on the border and trust border agents not to screw it up, even though they often did. Crimes still occurred, but most of them were handled by the police. She kept on patrolling, regardless.

She ended this particular patrol in New York, just in time for the interview circuit.

TWO

"ANCIENT MARINERS WOULD caution sailors of troubling seas with the warning, 'Here Be Dragons,'" said Ray. "Here in the U.S. of A, we know that Here Be Dragons, all right."

It was a cheap laugh, and the studio audience didn't disappoint with a mix of laughter and cheers.

Ray tried not to frown at the teleprompter. He'd gone on vacation and missed the writing meetings, so now he had an entire script full of historical misinformation and bad jokes and not enough time to make edits before airtime. Nights like these made him wish the show wasn't called "The After-Hours Show with Ray Boyer" and had some other poor schmuck's name in it.

At least he was allowed to conduct interviews the way he wanted. Speaking of which, he was getting a thumb's up from Carry, his producer. It was the signal that his next guest was ready and waiting.

Ray straightened in his chair. "Ladies and Gentleman, here be the dragon herself – Cayna Maren!"

The band struck up the guest-intro music — predictably, "Great Balls of Fire."

The audience went mad.

She walked onto the floor. Boots, jeans, a simple blouse and looking deadly as ever. That wasn't hyperbole. Cayna's arms were relaxed at her sides, but she was flexing her fingers as if imagining turning her nails into claws and sinking them into nearby vulnerable necks. And the way her eyes slid from one face to the next, taking in the crew, the audience, and finally Ray, made Ray very certain she knew exactly where everyone was and where everyone went in relation to her.

She didn't seem to pay any attention to where the exits were, but then, she didn't need to. Ray had seen the footage from Pearl Harbor in World War II. She'd torn through those Japanese planes like a football team running through a paper banner. And then there were the videos filmed in 2001 that day in September, when Cayna had torn off one of the engines of the first airline flight, sunk her claws into the fuselage, and carried the 767 to JFK Airport, then repeated the whole thing seventeen minutes later with the second 767.

Cayna could make her own exit, if need be.

Ray had known her for the decade he'd been a talk-show host. He found it very easy to talk to her, but when she was around, a side of him always wanted to run until he found some hills to hide under. And yet, he'd still been the idiot to make small talk with her on the Miami beach last week. Maybe he did have a death wish, after all. His wife had accused him of that after he went diving, also last week, in an area known for shark sightings, but Ray had a feeling the sentiment could apply to this situation, too.

They didn't shake hands. Cayna didn't shake hands, period. It was a human custom she'd never picked up, or so she'd claimed in another interview long ago.

"Hello, Ray," she said with a smile. "How's your tan?"

"Well, as you know, I got a little sunburned last week on the beach. I want to thank you again for letting me borrow your bottle of sunscreen." He reached under the desk and pulled out the bottle. "And because I used some of it, let me just give you this pack of lotions for any other people who come to you needing help dealing with a sunburn." He picked up a basket full of bottles and tubes.

She accepted it all with a closed-lip smile. "I'm of course happy to help. It's why I'm here." She set the basket down on the seat next to her.

"Yes. I suppose that's true. It was a weird coincidence, running into you down there."

"Not really. I didn't know you were vacationing down there, but I went up and down every beach in Florida last week."

"What? All of them?"

She nodded. "From Perdido Key to Fernandina Beach."

"I … don't know where those are."

"They're near Pensacola and Jacksonville."

"That's a lot of beaches."

She laughed. "I was patrolling for the most part, not swimming."

"Speaking of that. I didn't know you were such a strong swimmer. You must have held your breath for twenty minutes."

"Well, as a dragon, I can hold my breath for long periods of time. I need to be able to hold lots of oxygen in my lungs to fuel my flames. I can use that oxygen store to hold my breath underwater for as long as forty minutes."

"Wow." That was … pretty impressive. Even after ten years of interviews, she still hit him with these new things about her. Dragons — or *this* dragon, at least — were complicated creatures. He never got tired of these moments, death wish or not.

She glanced away from him and smiled sadly at the floor. It was the first time she hadn't met anyone's eyes since entering the room.

Ray frowned.

"I've always loved the beach," she said. "Did you know 'Maren' means 'of the sea'? There's a reason why those ancient mariners you mentioned believed the sea was full of dragons – my clan may have been the flying kind, but we always admired our water brethren."

Ray's attention sharpened. "So, there are such things as sea dragons? And not just the small, seahorse-like kind I've seen in aquariums."

She shrugged. She focused back on him, and her neutral smile from earlier returned. Whatever memory lane she'd just been down, she'd taken the first exit out of it. "I've never seen one myself. Evidence suggests they existed once, but they seem to have gone extinct. No chance of a sea dragon becoming a second protector of American soil, I'm afraid."

"Well, you do a great job of it on your own. Doesn't she, audience?" Ray asked the crowd, who obligingly cheered and hollered.

"Speaking of," he said, "you're coming up on the hundredth anniversary of protecting this country."

The crowd went wild again, this time in more enthusiastic appreciation. But, hey, everyone loved a party, didn't they?

Sometimes, Ray really felt like he'd been doing this for way too long. His thoughts were becoming a little too cynical about every aspect of this job. Other hosts could keep going for fifteen or twenty years. He wasn't so sure he'd make it that long before he snapped.

"That's right. There's a centennial celebration planned four months from now, during the opening ceremony of the Olympics," Cayna said with that big smile.

"From all reports, the celebration sounds like it's going to be pretty special. Is there anything you can tell us about it?" Ray asked.

Cayna shrugged. "I'm not part of the planning. I won't go to any rehearsals until next month. I'm the wrong person to ask."

There was something off about her tone; something a little too plastic about her smile. And Ray, knowing full well they had two minutes left and his producers wanted him to keep all of tonight's content light, just couldn't help it. He had to ask the question that was suddenly the most important one he could ask.

"You don't sound so excited about it," he said. And then, the question, "Are things going okay as the dragon protector?"

If she was startled by the question, she didn't show it. "Everything's been pretty good. It's just hard to believe it's been a whole century. It's been pretty eventful."

He had the feeling she wasn't paying much attention anymore. How many interviews had she done today? There was just something about her tone that reminded him of other guests on an interview circuit. They would answer any question he asked with a by-rote answer, and he'd have to think on his feet and dredge up an unexpected question, just to get them to engage with him in any meaningful way.

"I thought dragons didn't think a century was a particularly long time," he said. "That's what you've told me before, that you guys tended to measure time in, what was it? Hundred-fifty-year gaps?"

This seemed to take her by surprise. He had no idea why this line of questioning was what did it, but he was glad, regardless, as she seemed to focus back on the here and now.

"That's right. Huh. I'd forgotten I told you that." Cayna frowned. "You know, I just remembered something. I'll be turning a hundred and fifty myself the same month as the hundredth-anniversary celebration."

That got a mixed reaction of surprise and cheer from the audience and from Ray, too. If she were human, he would have assumed she was in her thirties. Then again, she'd appeared thirty-something when he first met her, and she'd appeared to be thirty-something in photographs and videos filmed decades ago.

He'd known she was older than anyone else he'd ever met, but to hear her say it was something else. But, more than that, as the implications set in, he realized something that made him a bit troubled.

"Well, happy birthday," he said.

She gave him a warm, closed-lipped smile. He'd never seen her teeth, which was probably a good thing.

"Thank you," she said. "But I wasn't born. I hatched."

"Well, happy, um, hatch day? Happy hatch day."

She laughed. "Thanks."

"So, if you've been the American Dragon for a hundred years, that means you were fifty when you started."

"That's right, I was." She glanced down at the floor again. "I'd forgotten I'd been so young."

The audience laughed.

"Hey, that's young by dragon standards," Cayna told them.

"Yeah, it is," Ray said. "You would have been, like, the equivalent of a human teenager, right?"

Cayna wasn't smiling. She met his eyes. She seemed … unnerved? Was that the right word for a creature as powerful as her? As if Ray had caught her off guard?

"Not quite," she said. "If I'd been ten years younger, maybe. But at the time, I was an adult, by dragon standards, although some of the elder dragons had certain opinions about my maturity level at the time."

She seemed to think about it. "I guess I was transitioning from adolescent to adult. Like you pointed out, dragons mature at a slower rate than humans. Each change could take years. As a result, it's hard to pinpoint when exactly a dragon enters adulthood."

"Why on Earth would you become the country's protector then? Were your parents involved in that before they disappeared?"

"Oh, it's a long story," she said cheerfully. Her fake smile reappeared. "Ask me next time, and maybe we can go into it then."

He blinked. He glanced at the clock and realized their time was up. Carry was making an urgent "wrap it up" signal.

"It's a deal," Ray said, also cheerfully. He turned to the cameras. "We'll be right back."

"Nice going, Ray." Cyndy was not amused. She tapped a drawing pencil on her thigh. That was always her tell when something was bothering her. She pushed back her blue bangs and gave him an annoyed look; those were Ray's other clues.

"What did I do?" He dropped on the couch next to her. There were commercials playing on the TV, but at this time of night, the only thing she'd be watching was that night's broadcast of *The After-Hours Show*. Susie, too; their teenage daughter was rummaging around in the kitchen, but he had no doubt she'd been in here, too, while the show was on.

"You upset Cayna." She poked him in the arm with the pencil. "I like her."

"You like the dragon lady who could torch us all if she wanted to?"

"Cayna wouldn't do that," said Susie as she walked back into the room. It was Friday night, so she was allowed to stay up this late. She didn't always want to watch the show, but tonight was apparently the exception, probably because Cayna had been one of the guests. Susie curled back up in the armchair next to the couch. "She can't. The binding keeps her from harming any American citizen."

"Binding? What binding?" Ray asked.

"You know, the binding? The one everyone's celebrating in July?"

Ray and Cyndy exchanged baffled looks.

"Are you talking about the anniversary of Cayna's time as a dragon protector?" Ray asked.

"Well, yeah," said Susie. "Don't you guys know how it all started one hundred years ago?"

"I don't know. I think I may have heard a different story."

"Me, too," said Cyndy.

Susie exhaled in exasperation. "Cayna liked to go swimming on this beach up in Maine. A local fisherman struck up a friendship with her. But one day, he was sitting out on an outcropping of rocks, and when she flew down to meet him, he painted some runes or something on the rocks, and these runes or whatever bound her to the land. They made her protect the whole country. She only does it because of the spell, which won't let her hurt any Americans or any people peacefully visiting the country."

"Humans can't do magic," Ray said.

Susie shrugged. "That's the story I heard. And I think it's the real one. So, yeah, that means humans can do magic."

Silence fell for a moment. On the TV, Ray's face reappeared as he introduced his next guest.

"Yeah, that's definitely not the story I know," said Cyndy.

"What did you hear?" Ray asked her.

"Well, dragons like gold. So, the government offered Cayna all the gold in Fort Knox in exchange for her help defending us."

Ray considered this. He shook his head. "Nah, the U.S. didn't stop using the gold standard for a few years after that. No dragon would let us keep using gold as a basis of our currency if the government had just handed over that same gold to the dragon."

"So, what version did you hear?" Cyndy asked him.

"I heard that Cayna struck up a deal with the Woodrow Wilson administration. They agreed to give her an unlimited expense account in exchange for her being the dragon protector."

"You guys are way off," said Susie. "It was the binding. No dragon would ever care about a job. And I don't think they're that crazy about gold, not like the dragons in the Middle Ages."

"I don't know. I don't think I like the idea of the binding." Cyndy frowned. "If it's true, it means Cayna's here against her will, like a prisoner."

"Or a slave," Susie said.

"No. That can't be the truth. She's never given that impression, when I've spoken to her," Cyndy said.

Ray knew what she meant. Cayna was the perfect diplomat on every talk show and at every social event, like the ones Cyndy had attended. If Cayna was unhappy, no one ever saw it.

But Ray knew a fake smile from a real one, even on a dragon, and he'd seen Cayna's fake smile at every occasion.

"Well, we can't all be right," he said.

"None of us have to be right at all," Cyndy pointed out.

"You should ask her next time, Dad," Susie said.

How could Cayna have forgotten her age? She hadn't thought about it at all. She had a policy not to tolerate human birthday celebrations. No one had any incentive to remind her. Not even her PR manager mentioned it during her weekly check-in the day after the interviews.

If Cayna still lived with her clan, a century and a half would be the first major milestone of Cayna's life. Dragons could live for hundreds of years, sometimes over a thousand. Such a lifetime would be hard to quantify in human terms.

It didn't matter. Nothing of dragon culture mattered here in the United States, not when she was the only one around who knew anything about it. Her clan had disappeared long ago. Most humans thought Cayna was the only one left, but they were wrong. They were wrong about a lot of things.

She took to the skies, abandoning another hotel in a string of a million of them. She rarely spent the night in the same place two nights in a row. She'd only do that in a place she considered home.

She left Manhattan behind in moments and beat her wings against the wind. She didn't feel like gliding; she felt like moving. If she flew until she was exhausted, she wouldn't have dreams again tonight. Flying against the wind was a good way to start.

She was supposed to scan the skies and the ground for any threats she could intercept from the air. But today seemed to be another relatively peaceful one in a long, long string of them. Frustrated, yearning for some sort of action, Cayna just kept on flying. She wished she had a destination in mind.

What good was it to be a protector when there was nothing that needed protecting? If she only had a pile of gold to sit on like one of the dragons of a long-ago time, she could have depended on would-be thieves coming *to* her. Instead, she had to seek out danger, but a dragon protector of a country with one of the mightiest militaries in the world didn't have to deal with home-front threats. Really, a dragon was overkill; Cayna could see that clearly.

Cayna shook herself from her thoughts, startled. She hadn't realized just how long her thoughts had been wandering. She really should have been paying attention. A distracted dragon who was getting horrible sleep apparently didn't stay alert. A distracted dragon would, apparently, fly to the last place in the country she wanted to be.

The peninsula had always looked to her like a dragon's head, if that head was missing half its snout. Beyond it, across a small body of water, was Canada. The peninsula lay on the American side of the border.

Forest covered three-fourths of it. A paved road passed through that forest, connecting the mainland to the red-and-white striped tower of the West Quoddy Head Lighthouse.

It was bad enough she'd been having dreams of nests. It was bad enough that she was letting herself become distracted in interactions with humans and letting things slip she'd never told anyone. Why had her subconscious brought her here? Why now, of all days?

She landed on the dragon's throat, on an outcropping of rocks out of sight from the lighthouse. A posted sign told her: Gulliver's Hole; No Swimming / No Fishing. Pebbles shook loose under her claws, skipped across larger stationary rocks and tumbled into the bay. She tried to adjust her footing, but the rocks were slippery. With an unhappy growl, she tried not to move too much as she looked around, taking in the rest of the rocks, the path with benches just beyond the outcropping, and the tree line behind the walking path.

Once, the view from this peninsula of the Gulf of Maine and the Bay of Fundy had been her favorite. Grand Manan Island lay to the southeast, bigger and covered in more wildlife than West Quoddy Head. It was too far away to see from the ground, but it would take only a few wing beats to reach it. She remembered the journey vividly as if she'd made it yesterday, not a hundred years ago. She could taste the fish in the waters on her tongue. She wished, suddenly and yearningly, that she could fly across the Quoddy Channel. But Manan Island was a Canadian island, and she couldn't pass over America's borders freely, not anymore.

And the reason for it all, the reason she was bound to this land in the first place, was hidden in the slippery pile of rocks under her feet.

Cayna hadn't been back here since the binding. She thought she'd be able to sense the magic, but she couldn't. The runes were hidden in a crevice or under a boulder, out of sight even from her sharp eyes.

She hadn't thought about the binding in decades. When had she become so accustomed to her situation? When had she accepted it completely? When had she stopped counting the years?

It wasn't in the forties, when she'd torn apart Japanese fighters like they were nothing. She remembered resentment and anger, both at the Japanese for invading and at Roosevelt for granting her permission to cross international waters to reach Hawaii. It was the only way she could step out of U.S. territory, thanks to the binding. Oh, how she'd loathed having to ask for that permission. She'd been unable to enjoy the sheer amount of water spread out below her — a sight that had become an impossible one since the binding — and the reality that she couldn't enjoy it had further fueled her anger.

She'd already been in Southern California when news of the attack had reached her, but the flight across the Pacific had still taken almost too long. She'd flown at her top speed, far faster than was typical for her, but it hadn't been enough. She'd spoken a few words of magic to move even faster. She'd arrived barely in time to take out her anger on the second wave of retreating Japanese bombers.

And then she'd spent the rest of the war patrolling islands in the Pacific, protecting American forces. Each time she crossed the open water to a new island, she couldn't leave the new island until Roosevelt and then Truman gave her permission to cross international waters again.

Throughout the war, Cayna ricocheted between relief over having new territory to explore, irritation at having less distance to fly in, and frustration that she couldn't take out her feelings on invading forces more often. Too many times, battles happened on open waters where she couldn't reach. And yet, even though she enjoyed finding the occasional outlet for her rage, those outlets never tamed her ire at being treated like an attack dog.

But that was many decades ago. In 2001, when she'd saved the World Trade Center, her old loathing toward the president and toward the binding had been completely absent. Her rage hadn't been directed at the United States for forcing her to help them. Instead, she'd felt rage at the terrorists who'd dared to harm thousands of people she now considered to be hers. And she'd mourned and raged with the country when she'd arrived too late to stop Flight 77 from hitting the Pentagon or Flight 93 from crashing outside of Pittsburgh.

In the present, people were approaching the rock outcropping. She could hear them talking to each other. Cayna decided she'd been here long enough and took off.

She flew southwest until she reached the Big Bend area of Texas. Exhausted now, she didn't bother trying to get a hotel. She didn't think she could handle doing any small talk right now. Humans loved small talk too much.

She found a deer, flew to a plateau, roasted the deer with her own flame, and feasted. Then she found a dry, rocky cliff to curl up on. She tried not to compare it to the wet, rocky shore she'd left behind halfway across the country.

"So, *The After-Hours Show*'s Olympic Special is going to air at 5:00, an hour before the Olympics' opening ceremony." Carry looked around the table. "But we'll be filming in the morning at 10:30 at St. Luke Theatre."

Some people made notes on their tablets or notebooks. There was a lot to do in the three weeks until then, and they had regular shows to produce in the meantime, too. Everyone had already grabbed a donut or three from the box on the side table.

Ray said, "Who are the guests?"

Carry shuffled through her notebook. "Cayna Maren is scheduled, and she's agreed to our special requests."

"'Special requests?'"

Aaron swallowed his bite of a crème-filled. "We want to do an interview with her in dragon form."

Ray was surprised. "But she can't talk while in dragon form."

"No, she can," said Carry. "She doesn't do it often anymore, but she has in the past. I've seen some old footage of her doing it. It's ... spooky. Her voice echoes. But her dragon side is the side that the American public doesn't see often up close."

"Yeah, usually she's flying high up in the air if she's in dragon form," said Marcus.

"When you say 'echo'...?" Aaron gave Carry a curious look.

"I'll send you links to the clips," she said. "She can project her voice, but it's intense. It's like it bounces off the walls. Even outdoors. And there's this ... boomerang effect. Like her voice sounds close to you, then sounds distant, then comes back."

"We can incorporate something into the set design to muffle some of that effect," said Aaron, "if I'm understanding you right. Can't we, John?"

John nodded. "Or we could even enhance it. But we should definitely see those video clips first."

"Hi, Willow." Cayna walked into the room and gave the petite redheaded woman sitting behind the desk a warm, closed-mouth smile. Humans never liked it when she showed teeth. She tried not to upset the humans she liked, and she did like Willow Rosen. Willow wasn't the first PR manager Cayna had ever employed, but they'd been working together for five years now. Willow knew to schedule a batch of interviews all at once, never for longer than two days, and with at least three months between batches. She understood that the rule about calling Cayna once a week meant *only* calling once a week. She was, in general, pleasant to talk to.

"Hello, Cayna." Willow's smile seemed to contain every tooth in her mouth. It wasn't threatening in the slightest. Humans could pull that off. Dragons never could.

As Cayna drew close to the desk, Willow handed Cayna a stack of opened letters. "Here's the fan mail that I couldn't answer with a form letter. Oh, except for these." She reached across her desk for another short stack. "These are all from fans who want you to send them a foot print."

Cayna eyed the stack. At least it wasn't very thick. "Really? That's still a thing?"

"That group of fans that thinks you should have a star in Hollywood for some reason is still going strong. I don't know why they think covering your foot in paint and pressing it against a piece of paper is the next best thing, but maybe they think you enjoy it." Willow raised her eyebrows questioningly.

"No. Send them an apology letter. I'm not doing that anymore. Enough is enough."

Willow shrugged. "Sure thing." She dropped the stack back on her desk.

Cayna headed across the room. Most of the room was wide open and empty. It was a former dance studio with a high ceiling, just big enough for Cayna to shift, if she wanted. Besides Willow's desk, the only other furniture was a small table and a couch shoved against the wall near the door. The floor had a new rug on it, Cayna noticed. The new one was plain blue. It covered the entire room, even a deep gouge Cayna had accidentally left in the wooden floorboards once. Only one piece of art hung in the room – a large painting of a beach scene, which Willow had bought and installed herself. The painting conveniently covered an old scorch mark on the wall behind it. A row of tall windows behind Willow's desk were covered by curtains for privacy. The last thing Cayna wanted was paparazzi bothering her when she made a visit to the office.

She kicked off her sandals and stretched out on the couch, still in her human form. She shuffled through the letters. Some of them were handwritten, while others were printouts of emails. The recipients seemed to vary in age. None of their queries repeated questions she'd heard in interviews in the past half-decade or so. She approved. Cayna grew so tired of repeating herself after a while. Willow always did her research in that regard and seemed to be particularly talented in keeping Cayna interested in playing the PR game.

Cayna reached for the laptop on the table and started composing answers. Three letters in, she paused. "Willow," she called across the room. Her voice echoed off the walls and ceiling, but in the ordinary way that human voices echoed in a large space. "Where did this one come from?" She held up a lined piece of paper covered in handwritten script. There was no signature, but something about the handwriting seemed familiar. Some fans wrote to her often, so it was probably one of them, but it was odd that they hadn't signed the letter.

Willow shuffled through a group of envelopes. "Nova Scotia. The return address doesn't have a name. It's just a PO Box."

The handwriting clicked.

Dor sent the letter. Doryu Maren. Dor. *Her* Dor.

She sat up. The urge to change rose. In a matter of seconds, she could throw open one of the windows, stretch her wings, soar to any of the taller towers in the city, call out to her nest-brother and wait for his answering call —

— but she stopped herself. This letter wasn't a calling card. It hadn't been sent ahead of Dor's arrival in

New York. No, the clan wouldn't come back. When she'd been bound to the country, they'd gone into hiding. She wouldn't want it any other way, no matter how much she missed them.

No, her nest-brother took enough of a risk sending her a letter. Why on Earth would he leave a return address? That seemed the most reckless of all.

Willow would have thrown out a letter without a return address. That had to be why.

"Dear Cayna," said the letter in Dor's pointy handwriting. "My two friends and I are either graduating soon or have graduated recently. It's been like a rite of passage for us, and it feels like we're starting a whole new chapter of our lives. We were wondering if dragons had any graduation ceremonies or rites of passage that humans don't have. If you do, what's the ceremony for, and what changes does it bring?"

Cayna ran her human fingers over the penned sentences. It was so hard to write in dragon form. She could just imagine Dor's coal-colored, human-form hand holding the pencil. None of the words actually touched the lines printed on the paper. Every letter fell between the blue lines, even the bottom tips of the Gs and the Ys and the Ps. She'd forgotten he did that. He was a bit OCD about it actually, if OCD even existed in dragons.

On the surface, the letter was vague and a little nonsensical. The "two friends" had to be code for Dor's and Cayna's mates. The four of them had allied together to share a nest so long ago. They'd cohabited for such a brief time before the binding forced them apart. So many of her dreams lately had been of them.

But dragons didn't have graduation ceremonies, which meant the graduation part of the letter was also in code.

Was Dor talking about turning a hundred and fifty? He was the youngest of their nest and wouldn't reach that age for another seven years. Cayna was the second-oldest. She couldn't think of any other "rite of passage" her nest-mates would be experiencing right now.

Dor knew what the one hundred and fiftieth birthday meant to dragons. He didn't need Cayna to spell it out for him. So, why did he want her to think about it? And why would he want her to think about what happened *after*? Nothing much happened after, and not a whole lot happened during the birthday, to be truthful. It was a milestone, but a dragon didn't get special privileges like a human turning eighteen or twenty-one did. Well, maybe the dragon received more respect from the elder dragons, but that was about it.

Dragons over a hundred and fifty tended to have children. That thought just made Cayna sad and angry over things she hadn't been able to change in a century.

"Hey, you want to hear about the program for the Olympic opening ceremony?" Willow called to her. "The director has sent me the latest."

Cayna didn't care. But time went on, and this was her life now, letter or not. "No point." She folded up the letter, pulled her wallet out of her pants pocket, and pushed the letter inside the wallet. "They'll just change it a dozen more times before rehearsal next week."

"Not the bit where you come in. The contract I secured for that was very explicit about no changes close to the date." Willow looked smug. "And yesterday was the cut-off date."

Cayna matched her smirk. "Good job. All right." She stood up and stretched. "Lay it on me."

"Your part's actually pretty small, all things considered. There will be this big musical number to open the Olympics, where all the things the United States is proud of or whatever will be paraded around and sung about. Industries, Hollywood, landmarks, that sort of thing. The production will transition into a number recognizing your role as protector for a century. You'll walk in —"

"Walk?"

"On your smaller legs." Willow gestured to Cayna's currently human legs. "You'll be wearing a star-spangled robe or something. I gave them your measurements, but they'd like you to do a fitting at the rehearsal. You'll walk out to the stage, and during a key point of the song, you'll transform while in the process of discarding the robe. They'd like you to do that while staying PG."

Cayna shrugged. She could do that easily while maintaining delicate human sensibilities. She'd done it before.

"You'll then fly around the stadium. Like, you'll circle over the audience a few times. Then you'll land back on the stage. They nixed an earlier idea about having you set some props on fire. It's a health risk. Instead, you'll pretend to blow a flame, and a big firepit will erupt in flames. Controlled by them."

Cayna stiffened. "Who do they think I am, some idiot who throws a lit cigarette onto dry grass? I can control the size and direction of my flames just fine."

Willow held up her hands. "It was their decision, not mine. They wanted you to growl instead, but I told them no way."

Cayna relaxed a little and nodded in approval.

"At the big finish of the song, you'll fly out of the stadium. And that's it. Then the Olympics teams will parade into the stadium. They'll have a wrap-up song at the end, but you don't have to stick around for that."

"Okay, then." Cayna plopped back down on the couch. "You know, Willow, there are stories I was told as a hatchling of great feasts dragons would receive after helping the local populace out."

She glanced over to see Willow giving her an incredulous look. "Sure. Your clan must have had a very skewed idea of history."

Have had. Even Willow used the past-perfect tense or the past tense when talking about other dragons. Even *she* thought they were all gone and Cayna was the only one left.

The letter in Cayna's pocket told her differently. Not that she had ever doubted it. She knew how well dragons could hide. She was the only one who couldn't. The binding wouldn't let her disappear.

For a moment, Cayna thought about sharing the letter with Willow. Willow would have read it already, of course, but she was still in the dark about what it really meant. However, due to their frequent contact, she knew a bit more about Cayna than most humans got the chance to learn. If Cayna shed light on the situation, perhaps she, more than most humans, would understand what the folded piece of paper meant to Cayna. She could keep a secret, as well.

But Cayna quelled the urge. Willow wasn't clan, and clan loyalty — and clan secrecy — were more important. Clan secrecy kept the clan alive.

Willow was still talking. "Humans and dragons have always been enemies, according to the stories I grew up hearing. The only feasts humans held occurred after a local hero had slain the local dragon."

Cayna scoffed. "Those are just myths spread by the church during the renaissance. Dragons kept better records about dragon history. There were many times when dragons helped humans, in the old days, before I hatched."

"Huh. I think I like that version of history better, if it's true," said Willow. "But, anyway, if you're not happy with the ceremony, it's a little late to make changes. But we could hold a party afterwards. That wouldn't be a problem to arrange. Lots of people love you."

Cayna scoffed. "I hate human parties."

"Yes, I know. Which is why we didn't have one scheduled in the first place." Willow sounded exasperated, but when Cayna looked over, the human was smiling. "The only party you'd get anyone to participate in is a human one. You'd have a hard time finding anyone who'd be into the dragon idea of partying."

Cayna smiled sadly. She wouldn't have a hard time locating "anyone" at all. The problem lay in traveling to them. Dor knew that. Time may have passed since the binding, but nothing about it had changed. It made no sense to dwell on the milestone time had delivered to her. She burned with the urge to decipher the true meaning behind his message.

"You're telling me you wouldn't like the feel of the wind in your wings as you race against your opponents?" Cayna said teasingly. "I guess you don't like dragon-flame-roasted meat, either. Or wrestling matches using either your claws or your tail, but not both."

Willow laughed. "No, no and no."

Cayna laughed with her. She jumped to her feet. "I'm going on patrol, unless there's something else?"

"You haven't finished your replies." Willow gestured at the laptop abandoned on the floor next to the couch and the pile of letters on the table.

There was no way Cayna was going to sit still any longer that day. "I'll finish them next week."

"All right. See you later."

Nonstop ads for the Olympic opening ceremony played in Times Square. In them, Cayna in her scalier persona flew from one screen to the next and then seemed to fly at the viewer before soaring away. She was a highlight of new TV and internet ads, as well.

Ray hadn't expected to learn anything more about how Cayna became the dragon protector of the United States. But as her hundredth anniversary drew closer, she entered more and more of the interactions Ray had each day with crew members, various guests on the show, and even the New York cab drivers that took him to and from the studio. Everyone wanted to complain about the traffic the Olympics would bring to New York, on streets that were already packed on a normal day. But they were just as open to talking about Cayna.

What he found surprising was that no one agreed on how Cayna became the American Dragon. Some people had heard the same stories that Ray, Cyndy and Susie had heard. But others had heard vastly different and ridiculous origin stories, things like:

— Cayna protected American citizens because she was proud to be herself an American, and she was just doing her part as a patriot to keep the country safe.

— Cayna was told that the U.S.'s gold had secretly been buried underground, and the government promised to tell her where to find it only after she protected the country for 300 years. All the patrols Cayna did were part of her search for the gold so she could break her contract before the 300 years had passed.

— Cayna had originally been President Lincoln's secret pet dragon and, after his death, she simply continued to protect the country that her old master had loved so much.

— Cayna was grown in a lab in the future and sent back in time. She protected the country because that's what she was designed to do.

One weekend, Ray sat at the table with his family and shared his favorite versions of the more bizarre stories he'd heard. "Has no one even asked her how she became the protector?" Ray asked Susie.

She shrugged. "I don't know. I guess not. It hasn't happened in any interviews in, like, the past seven years or so. I've watched all of those."

Ray thought about all the things he knew about the history of dragons. Most of it wasn't particularly happy. Dragons had played a vital role in many wars in the past, usually against their will, with human soldiers and warriors riding them into battle. That was before the Catholic Church decided that because dragons could do magic, they were evil. The church led hunts against dragons, treating them with as much barbarism as they treated women accused of being witches. They were a big reason why only one dragon existed today.

But his knowledge of dragons in the early twentieth century was a little too unclear.

Ray's younger daughter, six years old, wasn't listening to them. She was very clearly bored with the conversation. She blew a raspberry, propped her chin on her hand and ran her fork through a groove in the kitchen table.

"Rebecca, that's not how we use silverware at the table," Cyndy said.

Rebecca looked annoyed but set down her fork with a slam.

"Rebecca," said Cyndy.

Ray studied the groove his daughter had widened very slightly. He needed to put some sort of wax seal over that. The round wooden table was chestnut-colored, sturdy and well-made. Ray had found it at a garage sale years ago, long before he'd landed a spot in late-night television and bought the high-end house they lived in now. Despite that, it fit perfectly with the rest of the décor in the house. They'd owned the table for twenty-five years, and yet, he didn't know its origin any more than he knew Cayna's.

Maybe you get used to seeing something and you just don't think about how it got there, he thought.

Or maybe he was getting a little too philosophical over a piece of wood and he was reading way too much into all of this.

Later on, an impromptu backyard game of soccer/hockey – soccer with hockey sticks, which was harder than it sounded but fun – helped take care of Rebecca's restlessness. After the game, Ray asked Susie to show him the websites that talked about Cayna's binding. She showed him a couple of blogs that referenced ancient newspaper articles and an influencer's video that analyzed the story. None of it was what Ray would call "hard news."

He ended up sitting in his and Cyndy's room with his laptop. He tried a few Google search terms, looking for the newspapers. None of them were archived online. If he wanted more answers, it would require more work.

He always did research into the guests he had on the show. Sometimes, the interns did some of the research and gave him the gist. The rest of the time, he did it himself so he could be as knowledgeable as possible about their recent projects. It wasn't hard to pique his interest, and he would often become engrossed in whatever he found with only a smidgeon of digging.

But this felt different. It felt like he was cracking down on a genuine mystery. That just did not happen in the world of late night.

"You look like you've got something juicy," Cyndy commented. "Who's on the show next week?"

He shook his head. "It's not that. I'm looking for info about Cayna."

She sat on the bed and leaned over to read his screen. "Huh. You think there's something to Susie's theory?"

"I hope not." He closed the laptop. "But I won't know for sure until I can ask her. And that won't happen until the Olympics."

She shrugged. "Seems fitting for you to ask her about the beginning during the one-hundredth-anniversary interview."

"It could be."

THREE

A BURST OF steam fell from Cayna's nostrils. She dug her claws into the cement outside the Air Force hangar as she did an abrupt about-face. Bits of gravel chipped free from the grooves she scratched.

A passing airman had to hit the deck to avoid her tail. He looked up at her and cautiously got to his feet. Cayna huffed at him — a noise that sounded too impatient to be taken as an apology, but the airman lifted a hand and said, "Sorry," saving her the trouble of making a better effort to be sociable.

She continued to pace. Nearby, pilots all too calmly walked to their planes and went through pre-flight checks with technicians standing by. Cayna wished they would hurry up. She itched to get started on today's drills. Humans took so long to get in the air, forced to rely on machines that were too unreliable for her tastes.

She pondered over Dor's letter as she paced. Days had gone by, but she hadn't had as much time as she'd have liked to decipher her nest-brother's code.

She wouldn't have much time to think on it today, either. When she made another about-face, she noticed that a couple of officers had stepped out of the control tower next to the hangar and seemed to be heading her way. Whatever they wanted to speak to her about, it would ultimately mean a delay to getting in the air. Cayna huffed in annoyance and tried to remind herself to be patient.

Colonel Hardass and her faithful sidekick drew closer. Colonel Yara Reddington frowned up at Cayna. This was nothing unusual. The colonel seemed to have a permanent frown and an expression of constant disproval. Maybe she smiled, but Cayna never saw it. She was well-decorated and wore the proof on her uniform. Not only had she completed missions time and time again, she'd returned from each mission with a growing suspicion of everything around her.

That was, of course, only Cayna's impression. But she noticed that Reddington's gaze would be a little sharper and her comments more biting with each passing year that they'd known each other.

The younger Major Arthur Farris gave Cayna a nod. He was the embodiment of regulations, from his polished boots to his one-inch haircut. He was the consummate professional while on the job, but there were laugh lines around his mouth. He would break into a smile on occasion, although usually not when the colonel was nearby.

"Good morning, ma'am," the major said.

"Colonel, Major," Cayna said.

Her dragon-form's voice reverberated out of her throat. On the airfield, all sounds carried, but hers seemed to travel even farther away. It reached down into human eardrums and echoed off the middle-distance. Conversations halted. Nearby airmen glanced over. Instead of fading away, the echo seemed to be closer, just feet away. The second echo was far, far beyond the end of the airfield, but the third echo made some of the younger officers doing flight-checks turn in their seats or look over their shoulders, searching for the person who'd just said, "Colonel, Major," in their ears and finding no one there at all.

The major tensed as if trying to hide it, but Cayna noticed him shiver. Colonel Reddington's only reaction was a tightening of lips. Out of everyone at this base today, the colonel had the most exposure to Cayna's voice.

"I understand congratulations are in order," Cayna said. She bobbed her head, which allowed the spike on the tip of her snout to point at the new medal decorating the major's jacket.

Her voice received the same reaction as before. But more people seemed to have figured out who was speaking. Most of the personnel on the airfield paused in their tasks to watch Cayna.

"Thank you, ma'am," said Major Farris.

"We have reason to believe that a hostile government has developed a projectile that can pass through a dragon's defenses," Colonel Reddington said.

"No human weapon can penetrate a dragon's defenses," Cayna said.

The expression on the colonel's face was almost a smirk. "Our intelligence suggests that it was created from sea dragon bone."

Anger burst from Cayna in an exhale of steam. She slammed her forepaws into the concrete. "The sea dragons have been in hiding for centuries! How could any human agency capture one?"

"We don't know," Major Farris admitted. "They do have two incomplete skeletons of sea dragons on display in museums. Both skeletons are mislabeled as Dracorex remains, but it's possible they've found a third corpse and have used it to create projectiles strong enough to rip through both dragon hide and magic shields."

"We'll keep you apprised as the situation develops," the colonel said. "But today, we'd actually like you to pretend the blanks firing at you are these projectiles. You need to dodge them, not just let them bounce off of you like you usually do. You're not indestructible." There was nothing but contempt in her voice.

"Understood. Thank you for the reminder," Cayna snapped.

"You're welcome," the colonel said.

"We just want to make sure you're prepared," the major said in a reassuring tone. Too many times, he'd had to act the part of a referee placing himself in the path of two pairs of moving boxing gloves.

The planes headed at last for the runway. Cayna didn't wait for them to enter the sky. She started her attack on them immediately, sending them scattering with their wheels still on the ground.

Cayna decided she disliked pencils. Pencil marks smudged too easily. She'd been forced to trace over Dor's handwriting in pen to preserve the message, and her penmanship was never as neat as his. She almost took a photo of the piece of paper, but caution ultimately stopped her. No one would dare search her pockets for a letter – she couldn't hurt pickpockets, but she'd torch their possessions in a heartbeat – but her phone was too easy to misplace. She didn't want anyone to wonder why she had a photo of an ordinary fan letter.

She spent her days on patrol or doing drills with the air force. It was all very routine, but it required her concentration. She read the letter again every night. But she still wasn't sure what Dor was trying to tell her. She felt frustrated. It would be just her luck that, at some point in the past century, Dor had learned something specific about a dragon's hundred and fifty-year birthday, and he'd forgotten she hadn't been there for that lesson, too.

On a Washington beach, she took advantage of her stronger eyesight and the lack of beachgoers at three in the morning. As the waves washed along the shore again and again, she settled down on the sand, transformed into her human form and kicked her backpack off her ankle. She didn't bother with clothes. She searched for a handy stick. She then proceeded to write in the sand with only moonlight to see by.

Sure, she could have changed into her clothes, gone looking for a hotel, and done this on a pad of paper. But she was far too frustrated by her lack of progress over the past month. She currently had no tolerance for humans. It was bad enough that, tomorrow, she'd have to spend hours rehearsing for the Olympic opening ceremony.

"150-Year Birthday," she wrote in the sand. Under it, she made a list.

"1. Celebrated by dragons, not humans."

"2. Dragon earns respect from older and younger dragons."

"3. Dragon is considered old enough to rear children."

Sometimes younger dragons had children, but that happened rarely. In American society, eighteen-year-olds were considered old enough to have children, although younger teenagers had them sometimes, too. But a hundred and fifty-year-old dragon wasn't equal to an eighteen-year-old human. The dragons were a little further along in maturity. At age eighteen, humans were considered legal adults, able to vote, able to enter bars, able to gamble, able to sign up for vacation giveaways, able to make decisions without parental permission. Dragons, meanwhile, started doing the equivalent of that around age forty or forty-five.

She considered the list for a minute. The air force drills had done nothing to calm her. She needed to do something, anything else, right now. She needed to think, but before she could, she needed to work off steam, figuratively and literally, seeing as how steam was pouring out of her human nostrils. She growled, threw down the stick and ran into the surf.

The water was ice cold. Each splatter of salt-infused spray made her shiver as it hit bare skin. The spray sizzled on contact with her breath. She dived and brushed against the sand on the bottom far too soon. When she resurfaced, she used her momentum to shift straight into a freestyle stroke. The waves crashed into her face, making her splutter and cough on gulps of salt water. In-between crests, she treaded water for a moment, sucked in a deep breath and clamped her lips shut. She held that breath for the next thirty minutes.

Pressure rose in her chest. Finally, she couldn't take it anymore. She released her breath and sucked in huge, greedy gulps of fresh air.

She let herself change. She'd swum far out, away from shore, but it was a quick flight back to land. She changed back to her human form and let the sand stick to her wet feet as she knelt over the list and picked up the stick. The air formed goosebumps on her wet skin as she considered the list again. The air was cold, but she felt clearer-headed now.

Strange that she felt clearer-headed after doing an activity away from the humans she was bound to protect.

She started a new list in another patch of sand. "Dragons / Humans," she wrote.

"1. longer / shorter lifespans."

"2. can / can't transform."

"3. magical / nonmagical."

She hesitated. She made an edit to that line:

"3. magical / nonmagical (mostly)."

She wrote down all the differences she'd ever noticed, and there were a lot of those. The list continued for several feet. But which differences were relevant? Was any of this relevant to Dor's riddle?

She paused. She reread the item she'd just written.

"104. get stronger / get weaker with age."

Dragons didn't suffer from old age. They gained glory from it. They exulted in it. As a dragon grew older, they gained strength. Their bodies became tougher and stronger. Their senses sharpened. They flew faster and farther without tiring. They became quicker and fiercer in battle.

A dragon could theoretically live forever, though no dragon had. No, their bodies didn't weaken like humans did. It was the magic that did in a dragon, eventually, if a fatal wound didn't do the task. All dragons had a natural resistance to magic. It was a strange quirk of their natures, but it was useful in battle against magic users. But that resistance to magic grew stronger over a dragon's lifetime, and it didn't distinguish between the dragon's magic and an enemy's magic.

As a dragon aged, shifting between forms became harder. Fire-breathing took more effort. And, eventually, a dragon would try to draw a fiery breath and fail, or a dragon would try to shift between dragon and human forms, and the pain would destroy them.

Cayna's own grandmother had died that way. Her body had stopped working after a failed transition from dragon form to human form. Cayna had never known her grandmother, but she'd heard the stories. Cayna's grandfather and her grandparents' nest-mates had grieved deeply for her, but they'd told the story of her passing with pride, because she had been a warrior until the end. She'd gone out furious, scorching the roof of her nest's cave through the night, until her lungs gave out, then her heart. Cayna had seen the blackened patches on the cave roof.

The magical resistance built slowly and steadily over a dragon's lifetime. It happened so gradually that Cayna hadn't noticed, yet, if it affected her own abilities to change or breathe flame. She probably wouldn't notice any discomfort until she was five hundred or so. Then she'd be able to go another four hundred or more years before it began to hurt to use dragon magic.

To live past a thousand years, all a dragon had to do was pick a form, never shift to the other one, never draw flame, and never cast spells. These things were integral to a dragon's life. Cayna had never met a dragon who'd managed to go without.

All of this flashed through her mind. She hadn't thought of any of this in so long. This was what Dor wanted her to remember. She felt certain of it.

A hundred years ago, Cayna had been a typical fifty-year-old dragon – as strong as her nest-mates, who were all around her age, but weaker than older dragons. But like other dragons her age, she'd been cocky. Her hubris had cost her so much. Because she'd been so young, she'd been the perfect target for the binding.

An older dragon never could have been bound. An older dragon would have been able to resist the magic. Dor was telling her to remember that she was older and stronger now. He was telling her that the binding's hold on her wouldn't last forever.

He was telling her it was time to fight it.

FOUR

"… SO, UM, YOU just fly in laps above the stands for the second verse. We'll have some fake flames and lighting effects that mimic flames on the stage and in the stands, and some spotlights will, uh, highlight your scales. Go about five miles an hour. That should be slow enough for you to do a few laps and for the lighting team to track you. During the chorus and third verse, you fly up and do some barrel rolls and other maneuvers in time with the music. Don't worry about the lighting, we'll have floodlights pointed at the sky that should help that. During the last chorus, you land on the platform — it'll be disguised as a rock outcropping, but it'll really be wood, so just, uh, remember that and land gently but dramatically at the same time. You pretend to breathe out a ball of flame, but don't really do it. We light some big flames in a pit in the middle of the floor. You go running and take off again and go soaring as fast as you can over the pit, fast enough that you put out the flames from the breeze. You fly up to the edge of the roof, land, look down on everyone. You could, uh, even dip down and stick your head into the closest occupied stands, just close enough to startle the audience. As the music crescendos in the big finish, you take off again and make your exit."

Cayna grunted. She stared with her human form's eyes at the stadium's playing field and stands. No clouds filled the blue sky overhead. The awning roof looked secure enough for her landing at the end, but she'd have to be careful lifting off from it so she didn't accidentally send bits of it falling onto anyone's heads. It would be a balancing act, because she wouldn't be able to dig in her talons for stability.

On the edge of her sight, the show director and his assistant director exchanged glances.

Willow cleared her throat pointedly.

Cayna homed in on her, then on the director, who blanched at the sudden attention.

"You said flames." Cayna stared hard at him. "I thought that was a safety issue."

He squared his shoulders. "Lighting them with electronic equipment has been okayed. As long as they're contained and don't come from an external source, we're good."

His accent sounded Eastern European, but which country, she couldn't have said. If she'd only traveled more before the binding, maybe she could have guessed.

Soon. Soon, she'd have the chance to see more of the

world.

"Fine." Cayna fiddled with the belt of her robe. "Let's get this started."

"Ten minutes," said the assistant director. And then she and her boss hurried away at a fast walk, leaving Cayna and Willow standing on the edge of the field.

"You look like you're worried about something," said Willow. "Anything I need to know about?"

Cayna just looked at her, distracted. "What?"

Willow frowned. "Okay, now I know I'm not imagining it."

Cayna felt annoyed with herself. "I'm just thinking about something that isn't important right now."

The lie came easily. When something had to do with the clan, she lied without remorse. But, oh, how she wanted to be elsewhere right now. She tried to focus on the here and now. She didn't like how distracted she was being, especially in public. It made her vulnerable, and it made everyone she was supposed to protect here vulnerable, too, something she still cared about due to the binding.

But she just couldn't seem to help being distracted. Nothing in her routine mattered after her epiphany two nights ago.

The director called out directions over the stadium's intercom to various crewmembers. Willow climbed up into the stands and took a seat. Cayna stepped further back into the grand entry until she was outside the range of any spotlights.

This particular rehearsal was solely about Cayna. She'd have to do this all again in a month, when everyone else in this ridiculous performance would arrive and be ready for a collective dress rehearsal.

The music began to pump through the speakers. Cayna walked out slowly.

The director paused the music and asked her to walk a little faster. She needed to be standing a quarter of the way between the entrance and the empty fire pit by the time the intro music stopped playing.

They started over. Cayna obligingly returned to her starting point and repeated the dramatic act of walking a few hundred feet.

As the song's instrumental section ended and the first lyrics reverberated through the arena, she began to change. She let the robe fall away from a body that didn't look human anymore, already covered in scales and clawed feet as her chin widened into a snout and her stomach expanded into a belly studded in natural armor. She could feel her tail take shape behind her, forcing her center of balance to shift. She bent down and set all four feet on the green. Her paws were bigger than any human head. The process took a second or two. Humans generally couldn't track it very well, so she knew she'd appear to be a blur to the crew watching her today. But the cameras filming the Olympics would pick up the changes, and their social-media uploads would receive a billion or more views as people at home slowed down the footage to see each frame.

In her dragon form, she filled the space before the fire pit. Cayna stretched out her wings until one of them provided shade above Willow, who gave her a thumbs up.

Cayna caught the eye of the director and the A.D.,

who were both staring at her with gaping mouths.

Cayna jumped up, above the green, beat her wings and began to circle the stadium, as directed. Crewmembers remembered themselves and tracked her progress with floodlights.

She had to fly at an angle, both to turn and to avoid hitting any stadium seats. But these were close-quarters, and she scraped a wing against a box seat's Plexiglass walls before pulling up slightly. A moment later, her other wing brushed against a sign hanging on a back wall and knocked it loose.

At the center of the field, wooden planks and platforms collapsed. The air stirred up by a wingbeat had knocked over the half-built set.

The music halted. The collapsing set became the only noise in the arena.

Cayna landed back on the field as the pile of wood finally settled. She growled, annoyed, at the director up in the announcer's booth.

"Take ten, Cayna!" he said over the speakers.

She rolled her eyes and flew straight up into the sky.

Above the parking lot, she circled the oval-shaped stadium, memorizing its layout almost automatically. She took in her surroundings, as well. South of MetLife Stadium, the Olympic ceremony's crew had set up a temporary village of cars and trailers, but the majority of the massive parking lot was empty. West of MetLife Stadium, across smaller parking lots and service roads, the jumbled buildings of the Meadowlands Sports Complex were quiet. At the north end of the complex, cars gathered around the race track. Horses pounded hooves around the bend of a track. Cayna was flying too far away from them to cause them to panic.

She noticed nothing suspicious in the area, which she didn't trust one bit. She'd have to double her patrols between now and the ceremony, both here and at the other stadiums and arenas reserved for the Olympic Games. No terrorists would be planting any surprises under her watch.

Cayna landed in an empty section of the southern parking lot. She changed into her human form and walked, naked, toward the stadium's southern entrance.

Willow pushed open one of the glass doors and jogged out to meet her. She held out Cayna's robe and turned her back — which was a bit amusing to Cayna — as Cayna took the robe and slipped it on.

"What would you do if you didn't work for me, Willow?"

The human seemed surprised by the question. "What, do you honestly think you're my only client? You don't give me enough work for that. I don't spend every moment at the office we use, either, you know. I've got another office that's cozier and not even close to being as drafty."

Cayna smiled. "Ah, of course. And what would you do with the time you spend working for me now?"

"I'd take on another client, I suppose. It would be hard to find another one as high-profile as you, but I think I could manage it." She seemed to really think about it. "I'd spend less time talking to military switchboard operators when scheduling your drills with SEALS and marines and airmen and so on."

Cayna laughed. It wasn't very funny — it was

probably true — but she laughed, anyway.

"I think I'd miss my conversations with the presidential aides," Willow said wistfully. "It hasn't always been, but since you-know-who left office, getting a call from the White House is a pretty nice boost to my ego."

Cayna laughed harder.

"Since you walked into this round of sharing," said Willow, "you seem awfully distracted. The last time I saw you like this was after that mass shooting in Florida four years ago. I have one question for you: Should I be ducking for cover?"

Cayna considered Willow, who met her serious gaze with one of her own.

"No," Cayna said after a moment. "You're perfectly safe."

Willow relaxed. She nodded. "Thanks." She glanced at her watch. "Those ten minutes are up. I'm surprised the A.D. hasn't come looking for us yet. She seems wound tight."

"It's just her flight reflex. It's natural for humans to feel it around me." Cayna considered Willow again. "Although your instincts have always seemed to be a bit dulled." It was one of the reasons they had a good working relationship. Cayna usually hated breaking in new people, because it took so long for them to get over the urge to bolt when she was in the room. She knew they couldn't help it, but it still grew tiresome. But Willow had never shown any fear around Cayna, not even during their first meeting.

"My so-called dull instincts are telling me that the

A.D. is about to bust through that door. Oh, look —"

The A.D. pushed open the aforementioned glass door. She waved at them and pointed at her watch.

Cayna squashed down her irritation, more irritation than the A.D. deserved. She wasn't really irritated at the woman. She was simply restless.

She'd spent the past two days processing and accepting the idea that she actually could leave. She'd been the American Dragon for so long that she'd stopped seeing it as a trap. She'd accepted her role here so fully that she'd stared into the future and had seen only this. She'd grown accustomed to the constant company of humans and lack of dragons.

One letter after decades of nothing had shattered all of her illusions. She was going to leave. She was going back to West Quoddy Head and she was going to try to break through the binding until she succeeded. Dor had told her it could be done, and she trusted him with her life.

But not yet.

She'd continue this charade of being America's friendly neighborhood dragon for a little longer. With the Olympics just around the corner, too much attention was on her. She'd need to plan her exit carefully. Soon, Cayna would see her clan again, and she would be free.

Cayna sat in a dressing room, waiting for yet another televised conversation about how excited she must have been to spearhead the Olympics with her big anniversary.

Willow picked up within three rings. "Rosen."

"Hi, Willow," Cayna said. "Look, I need a favor."

"A favor, huh? Other than the running around I've been doing all day, talking to the security detail for the Olympics, who keep changing their minds about where they want you during the games? Or the argument I had this morning with the director of Barclays, who didn't want to clear space on the roof for you to land if you needed it? Or the coaches I've had to shout down, who have demanded that their players have photo shoots with you?"

"You mean the sorts of things I pay you for? No, the favor doesn't have to be done until after the Olympics. I have something in a safe-deposit box in the old vault of the Sunset Lane Bank in Eagle Grove, Iowa. I just remembered it. I was wondering if you could get it personally."

There was a pause from Willow. "You want me to go to a bank in the middle of nowhere Iowa and get you something from a safe-deposit box. Sorry, Cayna, you don't pay me to run personal errands, especially not ones that require me to travel halfway across the country. You want someone to do that, I can hire you a personal aide."

Cayna laughed. She was going to miss this woman. "Okay, let me rephrase. It's not really for me. It's for you. A gift for being so amazing this week."

"Hmm." Willow sounded intrigued. "Well, that's different. That means I can have one of my own personal aides from the other office go get it."

Cayna laughed harder. "Have the Diplomatic Security Service and NYPD give me a call. I've got some concerns of my own about the detail. I'll give you the key and address to that lockbox when I see you tomorrow."

A knock came on Cayna's dressing-room door. "Two minutes," a voice said.

"Gotta go," Cayna told Willow. She hung up the phone and went out to play nice once again with the American public.

Willow was probably going to be pissed at her, later, after she disappeared. Willow was indeed putting a lot of effort into making the two and a half weeks of the Olympics as smooth for Cayna as possible. Hopefully, this little gift — a boxful of gold trinkets from the seventeenth and eighteenth centuries — would be enough of a bonus to make up for it.

Then again, Willow would probably be pissed all over again when she realized the Sunset Lane Bank had closed after the Stock Market Crash. It was now a restaurant, but the sealed vault had been deemed too expensive to try to break into and had been plastered over. The safe-deposit box in question was probably rusted shut, as well. But it was the best Cayna could think to do. When Cayna left, she had no doubt that the United States government would seize her assets, including Willow's last paycheck. After that, the only wealth Cayna would possess would lie in that box. She was confident Willow would be curious enough to convince the restaurant owner and the city of Eagle Hawk to crack the vault open again.

After the interview, Cayna left the studio on human legs and hailed a taxi driver stopped at a light. Traveling the human way in New York was often the easiest way of getting around, even if it wasn't the quickest. It saved her the trouble of having to find a place to land on each studio roof and saved her the trouble of dressing each time she changed forms.

It was all so routine.

When had this life become acceptable to her? When had she started to enjoy it? The binding had consumed two-thirds of her life. It would be foolish to believe it wouldn't affect her, but it had happened without her conscious consent, just like the binding itself.

The thought sent a burst of anger down into her core. How could she have let this happen? She was bound, a prisoner. Time hadn't changed that.

And yet …

Here she was, sitting in a taxi, only one of dozens of passengers in a cluster of plastic cars that her dragon form could have crushed under her feet. No one forced her to go to interviews. No one forced her to ride in cabs. No one forced her to do anything … anymore. She just went along with whatever humans wanted.

Decades ago, after the binding, she'd started cooperating with them for a number of reasons: out of a sense of curiosity and boredom, out of a growing desire to get to know her "charges" better, out of a growing pressure from journalists who kept hassling her for interviews.

These reasons seemed pitiful in hindsight. But she'd let herself believe it was worth it. Because she cooperated, she had privileges that no dragon had experienced in centuries. Perhaps that was why it had been so easy to let herself fully assume the role of Dragon Protector.

She remembered her life before the binding. She'd

hatched in a nest hidden on the side of a mountain in the Rockies. She'd spent decades traveling with her parents and their nest-mates, then with nest-mates of her own. They'd always hidden from humans, sticking to North American skies and forests and national parks away from human roads and cities. It had been difficult, it had been an adventure in a way, and it had been her life, completely hers.

The binding had changed things. She'd tried to hide after it was placed on her. But every time she saw a human in danger, she would interfere without hesitation. The binding would press down on her and force her to enter each conflict, whether she wanted to or not.

And so, she'd embraced a life in public. Partly because she had no choice. Partly to distract human attention away from her clan as they fled, going deeper into hiding because of what had happened to her. And in the process, she'd embraced the things she'd never been able to do before.

She could fly in the open.

She could leave evidence of her presence without being hunted.

She could interact with humans without needing to assume a fake identity.

These things often felt like freedoms. But they weren't. They came with heavy stipulations.

Cayna was allowed to roam around the country as much as she liked, but only as long as she performed her "duties" while she was at it.

She could show only aspects of herself, and only as long as she remembered human manners and behaved enough like them that they overlooked anything else she let them see.

That wasn't freedom.

She was pushed and pulled and ordered about. She was treated like a commodity, taken for granted because she'd been around longer than any human in the present had been alive.

She was a fool. Dor was right. He'd known she needed reminding.

She growled, low in her throat, a growl directed at herself.

The cab driver's head turned at the sound, but to his credit, he said nothing.

Her phone rang. Cayna scowled at it. Another human was contacting her, wanting something from her.

She sucked in a breath, and she released it as steam. But she would play the part they expected her to play, if only for a little while longer.

"Maren," she said into the phone.

It was a captain with the NYPD. "You wanted to speak to me about the security detail for this week?" he asked.

During the one-mile-long, twenty-minute drive, Cayna learned that the joint operation between the DSS, FBI and NYPD had finally made up their minds: Instead of having Cayna stay put in one spot, they wanted her in the sky constantly flying between all the locations in New York where games and competitions would take place. She'd keep an eye on everyone from the air. The officers and agents on the ground — and the regular security employed at the stadiums and gyms — would handle the rest.

He reassured her they could deal with "the rest," but she had him go over all of it, anyway. He started with the smaller arenas and related as many details as he knew about their rotations, security numbers, patrol routes and so forth.

The cab crawled slowly from one block to the next. It was a typical day in Manhattan, as far as Cayna cared to notice. But as the cab approached Times Square, she also noticed groups of people in matching uniforms. These had to be Olympic teams out sightseeing, no different than the thousands of tourists crowding the sidewalks in this area of the city.

Road traffic was as congested as ever. The cab driver didn't hesitate to ride the bumpers of every car and taxi sharing the road, and other cars did the same. Cayna had never bothered to learn to drive. But the New York City driver's mentality was one she could relate to. Nearly everywhere else in the country, drivers kept gaps between their cars, claiming it was safer. But "safe" didn't enter into a Manhattan cab driver's vocabulary. "Safe" was also not something dragons particularly understood, and Cayna was no exception. Cayna's cab driver cut into the next lane, quickly shifting into the space another car occupied, forcing that car to stop and let the cab in.

Despite everything, she didn't hate all humans. At least, not most of them. Individuals like Willow Rosen, Ray Boyer and even her cab driver were just fine.

Back when she'd been truly free, so few of her thoughts had been about humans. She suspected she'd go back to that mindset, if she could just break the binding.

On the phone, Cayna heard the captain say the words

she'd been waiting for, "MetLife Stadium."

"There will be eight guards on patrol at any given time," he said. "Operating in teams of two. One team will pass through each area of the stadium every twenty minutes, starting tonight. There will also be two additional guards watching the CCTV."

Twenty minutes. It was almost too good to be true.

"I'll be patrolling myself, double-checking all the venues tomorrow night and then again the day of the opening ceremony," she said. "Make sure your people know I'll be stopping by. We might as well get used to working together."

He agreed, and they hung up.

The cab entered Times Square, where the sidewalk traffic was the worst. On an electronic billboard, Cayna in dragon form blew fire at the viewer before flying away at top speed.

In the taxi, Cayna smiled. The ad was unexpectedly appropriate.

The humans who thought they could keep her under control deserved her rage. Instead, she'd given them her compliance. They were wrong to try to control her. It was time to face any human who thought dragons should be controlled.

They wanted her to perform for the world. She would show them what she could be if she wasn't forced to be their protector. She knew just how to send a message — to herself, to the governments of the world, to her hidden clan — all in one swoop.

It would be dazzling.

FIVE

CAYNA CIRCLED ABOVE the stadium, looking for unexpected flashlight beams and listening for suspicious noises. She heard none. Security for the Olympic Games was pretty good. Her absence would create a huge gap.

She dived into the arena and landed on the wooden platform at the center, the one the props team had finally transformed into a convincing fake rock outcropping, albeit one with a completely level peak. They'd made it extra sturdy, too, to serve as a landing pad.

She stepped off the fake rocks and onto the green. The arena and stands were semi-dark and empty. Some lights on the rigging were on, but the shadows were thick, and the stars above were easy to see. No guards had come running. She looked up in the direction she knew held a camera. She decided against waving at the person no doubt watching her from the security office.

What she was about to do would be the only message she'd need to send.

A huge metal fire pit stood between the stage and the exit to the locker area.   It was full of real firewood. Among the wood, she could see pipes where the flames would emerge. No doubt there were gas canisters under the wood pile, which would not be necessary tonight. She walked up to the pit and pawed through the wood, but the canisters weren't there. That was good.

She noticed that the seats in the lower stands were plastic. The seats higher up were nothing but aluminum benches bolted to concrete slabs, but the aisles were marked by shiny plastic strips. Between the plastic and the electronics throughout the stadium, it would be almost too easy to turn this entire structure into the biggest bonfire on the Eastern Seaboard. The stadium's sprinkler system wouldn't stand a chance of stopping it.

A deep breath in, a slight opening of her snout, and a release of pressure were all it took to shoot a thin jet of flame from her mouth to the pit. She could feel the heat on the roof of her mouth and on her tongue as the flamelight lit the arena. The firewood caught fire. The flames didn't go very high — there wasn't enough firewood for that — but it took only a moment for the fire alarm to go off.

It screeched in her ears, and she had to strain to hear beyond it for running footsteps and shouts. The guards were shouting at each other to get out of the stadium. She heard the clicking sounds of stadium doors being thrown open. She waited a beat, listening for more sounds, and heard none. The guards had left.

Cayna lifted into the air. She flew a few laps around the stands, allowing just enough time for the guards to get clear of the structure. She managed not to graze anything as she flew, not that it would matter in a moment.

Her flames licked seat after seat in row after row. Soon, every plastic seat was on fire. She spread a wash of flame over the aluminum and concrete seats, the walls, the awning, the lighting rigs, and anything else in the path of her fire.

Sparks flew. The flames spread. Every inch of the stands burned.

For her big finish, Cayna flew low over the untouched field. She unleashed another burst of flame. The grass burned faster than the rest.

She was surrounded by flames. The sprinkler system hadn't even turned on. The sprinkler heads were melting. The heat was searing, but against her hide, it felt marvelous. Smoke obscured the air like the sweetest-smelling cloud. Steel supports creaked and groaned as Cayna turned and shot for the sky.

Once clear of the stadium, she looked down. Below, fire trucks pulled into the stadium parking lot. Smoke climbed out of the center of the stadium. The structure began to shake. The fire trucks paused halfway across the lot. When the structure let out an ear-piercing screech, the trucks made an abrupt turn in the opposite direction. The drivers floored their gas pedals across the parking lot. Behind them, a section of the stadium collapsed. Flames and embers leapt as the walls gave way. Another section of the stadium dropped, then another. Safe at the far end of the parking lot, the fire trucks came to a stop. Firefighters jumped off the trucks and turned to stare as the conflagration blazed on.

Cayna climbed the columns of smoke and then kept going until she'd left the heat of the fire and the heat of summer behind.

The air around Manhattan was thick, as usual, with planes landing and taking off from airports. Just ahead of Cayna, a plane lifted its wheels off the runway at LaGuardia. Cayna accelerated and climbed higher, clearing the rising plane by about 10,000 feet. The atmosphere at 35,000 feet chilled her fire-warmed scales. Some remaining smoke exhaled from her nostrils as she coasted on an upper-atmosphere breeze. There was an American Airlines flight just ahead. She rose higher still, to 50,000 feet, to pass over it.

Her tail waved goodbye to Manhattan's skyscrapers, a dense cluster of steel to the southwest. The domestic sprawl of a dozen or more towns disappeared within a moment. She flew faster than she had in years. She wondered how long she had before they'd conclude, officially, that she was the one at fault for the fire. She gave it a few hours. Of course, men and women like Colonel Reddington would automatically assume Cayna was a suspect on the sole basis that a fire was involved. For once in the colonel's miserable life, the woman would be right about something. Time was on Cayna's side, but she would lose that advantage all too soon. The quicker she got to West Quoddy Head, the more time she'd have before the U.S. government caught up.

She soon came upon the suburbs and fields and forests of New York State, but it didn't take long to leave those behind for the suburbs and fields and forests of Connecticut, with Massachusetts already on the horizon. Clusters of electric lights marked the presence of cities and towns far below. Streetlight-lit roads and the security lights of suburban houses pockmarked the black masses of forests. Cayna could name every bright cluster of a city and every dark patch of a nature reserve. Off to her left, she spotted Worcester, Massachusetts; to her right lay Providence and Warwick, Rhode Island.

It would be difficult to avoid human air traffic completely, just as it would be impossible to avoid humans completely. She kept watch for the blinking lights of airplanes rising from regional airports. Hopefully, the commercial flights and air traffic controllers who noticed her would direct their planes around her, like they normally did, and do nothing else. Hopefully, the military wasn't paying close attention to the skies over New England.

The bright splotch of Boston spread across the far-distance, with a blanket of blackness beyond it. She itched to fly straight over the city, which would be the quickest route to West Quoddy Head. Instead, she banked west and skirted around the city in a wide half-circle. Tonight, she would steer clear of Boston Logan International, where 747s frequently took off from its runways toward the sky over the Atlantic. Soon, *soon*, Cayna would be able to fly those same flight paths and cross the Atlantic.

North of Boston, she followed the coast. For the rest of her flight, she kept the ocean under her. The United States claimed twenty-four nautical miles off the coast as their contiguous zone. Down in Miami, the zone thinned to three miles, but not up here in New England. Even with the binding still in place, it was easy enough to keep the ocean under her for the rest of her flight. She stayed close enough to shore to see city lights reflected on the waves near the beach. But directly below her, the ocean was too dark for even dragon eyes to see it. She was too high up to hear the waves crashing or smell the salt in the water.

She kept up her pace as she passed Portsmouth and Portland, and then she began to slow down and descend. She kept a sharp eye on the ground, looking for that uniquely shaped peninsula among dozens of tiny towns, islands and marshlands. America's contiguous zone narrowed near the border with Canada, so she banked to the north and traveled the rest of the way over land. She couldn't sense the United States-Canada border. She could never sense the border. She'd only know if she hit it when she came upon it. She'd hit it before. Contact always hurt, no matter how fast she was flying. She couldn't afford an injury, not on this night of all nights.

The peninsula appeared. She'd left behind the stadium only moments ago, but the journey had still gone far too slowly. She aimed for a break in the tree cover that was almost diamond shaped.

It wasn't quite big enough for her dragon form, and she broke a branch or two on the way down. With all four feet on the ground, she froze and listened. The noises of nature had paused. The creatures here had heard her coming and were keeping to themselves. She heard no human noises, other than the distant engines of cars driving along the road on the north end of the peninsula.

She shifted. Wings folded in and then disappeared. Thick, scaly legs became human limbs. Her stomach flattened and thinned. Her snout shrunk and turned into a human nose, mouth and chin. She went from being warm and comfortable to being a little cold.

She sucked in one heaving breath after another. The flight here had been bracing. On a normal night, she would have taken twice as long.

She had limited night vision, and her sense of smell wasn't particularly strong, unable to sense much beyond her own sulfur. But she knew where to go. She stumbled her way there, tripping over tree limbs and growling under her breath as her human feet fumbled through the underbrush.

The backpack was still strapped to the tree branch where she'd left it days ago. She'd tried to be stealthy that night. Hopefully, no soldiers were waiting for her at Gulliver's Hole tonight.

Cayna unstrapped the backpack, pulled out a change of clothes and shoes and dressed quickly. Feeling around, she found the plastic bag full of American bills and her turned-off phone. They went back into the backpack in exchange for a small mirror and a flashlight. She switched it on, pointed it at her head, and looked in the mirror. Her almond-colored skin and green human eyes were the same as ever, but her hair was no longer black. Instead, it was blonde. She'd dyed it hours ago. It was a relief to know that the dye stayed in her hair, even if that hair disappeared when she was in dragon form. She'd never experimented with hair dye before. She'd never had a reason to care. But the disguise might just come in handy now.

With her backpack slung across one shoulder, she aimed the flashlight at the forest floor and let it and the sound of waves guide her in the direction of the shore.

This almost felt like any normal day. She'd lost count of the number of times she'd had to find a spot of nature to transform from dragon to human and change into clothes. But adrenaline pounded in her veins, her heart was still racing from the flight here, and steam clouded the air in front of her every time she breathed out. She was primed for a fight. She'd ruined the Olympic Games, humiliated the United States Olympic Committee, damaged private property and gone AWOL from her responsibilities. She smiled. It had been so easy.

Forest noises arose once again, but not close by. Any animals in the closest trees were staying silent. The silence followed her as she hiked over tree roots and around foliage. She switched off the flashlight as she broke free from the trees. She found the path along the bank, easily visible in a flood of artificial light. The light shifted, leaving the path in deep shadow. The beam of light swept out into the water and toward the horizon. A second or two later, the lighthouse beam returned to illuminate the path, then swept back out into the water.

Cayna walked along the path, ready to duck into the trees at the first sign of a human. But no humans appeared before she reached the craggy rocks of Gulliver's Hole. She began to pick her way across the rocks, her steps guided by the intermittent, sweeping beam of the West Quoddy Lighthouse.

The runes were here, somewhere, hidden under loose gravel or under algae-slick rocks. She couldn't sense them any better than she could sense the border. But she'd find them.

SIX

"… THE PRESIDENT HAS called a state of emergency. A joint FBI and Interpol investigation was opened this morning. Known terrorist group ISIS is a lead suspect, along with Dragon Protector Cayna Maren …"

"… While the MetLife Stadium has been declared a total loss, the Olympic Games may still proceed in the other venues originally slotted for them. This includes the rest of the Meadowlands Sports Complex, which was not damaged in the fire. However, a temporary halt has been called to the games until the NYPD bomb squad and crime scene investigative teams can ensure that all Olympic Games locations are safe …"

• • •

"... I was in the security office, watching the CCTV footage, when I saw Cayna land on the green. We'd been told she would stop by at some point that night. But then she set fire to the set, and I knew that wasn't planned. And when there's a fire, procedure says to get all guests and personnel out of the stadium and call the fire department. So, that's what we did. Besides, when a dragon's on the warpath, you get out of the way."

"... The Olympics Committee will be holding a press release at four p.m. today to address growing concerns over whether the Olympic Games can continue as scheduled. In previous years, the Summer Olympics were cancelled on only three occasions, each time due to war. In 1916, World War I brought a halt to the games. In 1940 and 1944, World War II took precedent over athletic competitions. If this year's Olympics are cancelled, there is some speculation that the reason is because another war tantamount to a world war may be on the horizon ..."

At the beginning of the video, a man splayed his hands and opened his arms wide. "What's up, Terrans? It's me, Terrance." He sat back from the camera, revealing a hotel room in the background. His purple hair was puffy in the middle and shaved on the sides. "As you guys know, I drove to New York for the Olympics. Only, now it looks like the events I really wanted to see are being canceled."

An image of the blazing MetLife Stadium appeared, accompanied by an, "Oh, no!" cartoonish voiceover effect.

Terrance and his hotel room reappeared.

"Some of the competitions that were supposed to be held in the stadium are being relocated, but there are a few that still haven't found new locations. It's been a real mess here in New York.

"So, I went out for dinner last night, and I just happened to go to the same restaurant as a group of Olympic athletes."

The video cut to camera footage inside the atmospheric, dimly lit space of an upscale restaurant. The place was busy, but the camera focused on the middle of the room, where an Olympic team dressed in their team's matching jackets sat around a rectangular table, talking in hushed voices. They proudly showed off their country's colors, but they didn't look very happy.

"I had to look it up later, but this is the Women's Artistic Gymnastics team from Italy," said Terrance's disembodied voice. "They're here for an event that was supposed to be at the stadium, and they're still waiting to hear if they're even going to get to compete somewhere else."

The video returned to Terrance. "Man, that sucks, having to train for four years and fly halfway across the world, only to find out you may have to wait another four years.

"Terrans, this whole situation is not looking great. The authorities are still investigating all causes of the fire, but the footage of what appears to be Cayna Maren flying away from the stadium has been accepted as damning by some groups."

Terrance pointed a finger at the screen. "Well, I'm here to say that we shouldn't condemn Cayna just yet." He lowered his finger. "She's done nothing but help innocent people for the past one hundred years. Anyone who visits America peacefully has fallen under her protection. She's never destroyed public property before, so why would she start now? Something else is happening. We just have to find out what.

"Of course, the easiest way of clearing her name would be to find her and ask her what really happened. But she's been missing since last night. If anyone knows anything about her whereabouts, go to the link down in the description. It's up to us, Terrans. Let's find the only dragon in existence and clear her name."

"It's crazy over here." Carry's voice sounded hassled over the phone. "You should see the sheer number of uniforms running around and all the military vehicles on the streets. Traffic is even worse than usual, if you can believe that. Try to get to the studio as soon as possible. We've got a lineup of Olympians who want to talk about their side of this mess. We're looking at a possible two-hour special, at this rate. The network wants to fill the airtime that was supposed to go to the opening ceremony, and we're up."

It was 6 o'clock in the morning. Ray's wife and two daughters were still asleep, so he had the news on mute. He had a few news websites open in tabs on his phone, too. They all told the same story: The Olympics were in an upheaval after someone had set fire to MetLife Stadium in the middle of last night. The footage from the blaze was spectacular, with lots of smoke and lots of flames. He'd never seen steel melt before.

"What about Cayna Maren?" he asked. "Is she still coming?"

The American Dragon should have been in the thick of the investigation, on her own hunt for the culprits while coordinating with the FBI, NYPD, DSS, National Guard, Secretary of Homeland Security, or anyone else involved. She probably wouldn't have time to humor a talk-show crowd today, which meant *The After-Hours Show* would have a big segment of the show to fill at the last minute.

Carry laughed in disbelief. "Haven't you heard? She's the main suspect."

Ray said, "What? No way."

"Well, how many things do you know of besides a dragon's flame that can melt steel? There was no explosion, so there's no bomb involved."

"Ella! Stay close to me!"

Cayna jerked awake. She'd risen into a crouch on her human-form legs before she registered the noise that had awoken her. She homed in on the distant movement of humans on the path along the shore. They wore bright fabrics and walked in the sunlight, making them easy to spot, even with trees and underbrush between them and Cayna. One of them was much taller than the other, probably the man who'd shouted. A shorter, less-coordinated kid rushed ahead of him.

If civilians were allowed in the park today, that meant the authorities hadn't located her yet. That was good.

It was midday, according to the angle of shadows on the ground. About five hours ago, Cayna had curled up in this spot in the woods and slept half of the morning away. She'd shrunk to human form, choosing stealth over comfort. But the price of that was that her hair was full of knots and a couple of leaves, she itched like crazy, and her clothes felt grimy.

She'd spent five hours last night scouring Gulliver's Hole for the runes and found nothing. She could have sworn she'd scanned every inch of every rock and crevice. The runes couldn't be gone. A spell like the binding would keep the runes affixed to the rock, and no animals or water or accidental human interference would remove them. That was how the spell was supposed to work, anyway.

But all she'd found were a half-gone cigarette and a Milky Way wrapper.

When the sun rose over the horizon, she'd retreated into the forest. She was not, in any way, ready to give up. But she'd have to wait again for nightfall, after the park closed for the day.

Annoyed, frustrated, and feeling hungry enough to eat half a doe as an appetizer and an entire buck with its antlers as an entrée, Cayna scanned the nearby woods for prey but immediately abandoned that idea. She couldn't hunt here. It would be too noisy and too conspicuous. She had food in her backpack, which would just have to do.

She could go into Lubec, the nearest town, for lunch. But she shot down that idea. Any time wasted on traveling or interacting with the locals would be better spent here, close to her target.

Sticking close to the thing she coveted was a very dragon way of doing things, but when the soldiers came, she wanted to be able to defend her turf from the get-go.

Her phone had no SIM card in it. Its signal could be traced, so she'd left it behind. But without 3G, she was essentially blind to the outside world. She didn't like that, not one bit. Soon, she would need to go into town and find a WIFI hotspot.

She heard the father yell again. She peered through the scrub as the kid and her father headed northward toward the lighthouse.

Perhaps she could do recon without leaving the state park.

She stood up, stretched and took stock of her clothes. The shirt looked okay after she brushed off the dirt, but only as long as no one looked too closely. But when she discovered a long grass stain on her jeans, she sighed and reluctantly exchanged it all for her second change of clothes. She wouldn't have bothered, but she would be too noticeable if she walked into a group of humans looking like a homeless hitchhiker. So, she did the best she could to brush off the dirt, fixed her hair, checked her appearance in her pocket mirror, stuck on a pair of sunglasses and a hat, and made her way through the thicket to the path.

The path ran along the bank, curved into a half-full parking lot, returned to the bank, and ended on the lawn outside the lighthouse. The humans parking or packing their cars, walking along the path, and taking pictures of the lighthouse didn't pay much attention to her. With her blonde hair, sunglasses and hat, no one recognized her.

She counted thirteen visitors to the lighthouse today. There was no telling if her disguise would hold up within a larger population, but for now, it was perfect.

The grassy ground around the lighthouse sloped down to the rocks on the bank. Several paths had been beaten into the grass by human feet. She followed the footpaths. She used her phone to pretend to take a selfie with the lighthouse in the background, and she kept her phone out as a prop.

The brick tower of the lighthouse was brightly painted in thin red and white stripes. The wooden house next to it had windows on all sides, including windows in the attic, and a handicap ramp to the door. The windowpanes were dark. She spotted a surveillance camera mounted on the house. She kept her sunglasses on.

Tourists walked up the ramp and inside, but Cayna stuck to the outdoors, paranoid that the rooms inside would have cameras even if the exterior of the house did not. She did a full circuit around the picnic area, taking note of the woods on the outskirts of the clearing and the animals scurrying around within them. She noted the road that stopped outside the house, the scattered picnic tables, a brick utility shed, a seemingly random old bell, and a flagpole waving the flags for the United States, Canada and Maine.

She mistook a rough slab of granite for a headstone until she drew closer to it. Capital letters engraved in the granite proclaimed, "EASTERNMOST POINT IN THE U. S. A." Cayna thought that was unfair to Puerto Rico and the U.S. Virgin Islands. But it was true that West Quoddy Head lay at the easternmost point of the continental U.S. It was the easternmost point that she could travel — for now.

Cayna sat down at a picnic table. She stared out at the water as she dug into a bag of beef jerky.

A woman walked around with a selfie stick, paused a couple times, and raised her camera above her head. She seemed to be taking panoramic views of her surroundings instead of taking pics of herself, but what was most interesting was her outfit: a baseball cap with the rainbow-colored Google logo, paired with a neon-yellow vest over a regular blouse and jeans. She stopped near Cayna and paused to review the photos on the camera.

"Nice day, isn't it?" Cayna called.

"Hmm?" The woman looked up with a polite smile. "Oh, yeah, it is." She had a nose ring, Cayna realized.

"Do you work for Google?" Cayna asked.

"I do, yeah, for Google Earth. I'm just taking updated ground views of the lighthouse. Our current photos of this spot are a few years out-of-date, so ..." She shrugged.

"Has much changed since the last time Google took photos here?"

The woman considered their surroundings. "I don't think so. But Google likes to stay current as much as it can, anyway. And I like to travel, so I love it, personally."

"Ah." Cayna took a sip of her water bottle.

"What about you? What brings you here today?"

"Oh, just looking for some peace and quiet." Cayna waved in the vague direction of north. "I'm on vacation.

I'm staying in Lubec. It was either this or the Olympics, and since that stadium caught fire, it looks like I'm better off here, anyway."

"Oh, I know! Can you believe that happened? It was lucky it happened when the place was empty. Can you imagine what could have happened if the fire had started during the games?"

"That's true. I hadn't thought of that," said Cayna, who had thought in depth of what would happen if she'd started the fire during the opening ceremony. But that hadn't been an option.

If the binding wasn't in place, she wondered if she could have set fire to a stadium full of humans. She balked at the idea ... but was the binding influencing her reaction, or were those her genuine feelings?

Cayna focused on the here and now. "You think it was an accident?"

"Probably not," the woman admitted. "It happened a little too close to the Olympics for it to be coincidence, you know?"

Cayna nodded. "Maybe."

"Whoever's responsible, I can't believe Cayna could have done it."

The woman now had Cayna's undivided attention.

"The Dragon Protector? Why would anyone think she's responsible?" Cayna tried to sound incredulous without overdoing it.

The woman looked surprised. "You haven't seen the footage? There's a video going around showing what looks like a dragon flying away from the stadium while it was still in flames. And one of the stadium's security guards has come forward saying that Cayna was there just before the fire started."

"Oh," Cayna said. "You know, that sounds pretty conclusive to me."

The woman looked upset. "Maybe. But I don't want it to be true."

"What if it is, though? What if she's decided she's done being the American Protector? I mean, if I had to do the same job for a hundred years, I know I'd want a vacation. Maybe even a permanent one."

"That doesn't explain why she'd set a stadium on fire. Couldn't she just, like, quit if she doesn't like it?"

"I don't know," Cayna said, now a little irritated. This Google employee had a seemingly unshakable faith in her Dragon Protector.

Normally, humans paid close attention to Cayna's body language. Normally, her irritation would have been obvious and make most humans want to run. But the Google employee didn't know anything was amiss. It was amazing what sunglasses and dyed hair could do, as well as the human tendency to rationalize things that didn't make sense – like the thought that a dragon would be making small talk while having a picnic lunch at a national park. Cayna thought about removing her sunglasses, just for the shock of seeing recognition appear on the human's face. She had to restrain herself.

She plastered on a tight-lipped smile, remembering to keep her teeth out of sight. "Anyway, you're probably right. It's hard to believe Cayna would be so destructive, isn't it?" She picked up her trash and stuffed her uneaten food back into her pack. "It was nice talking to you."

The woman's smile was a little less polite and a lot

more troubled. "You, too," she said hesitantly.

Maybe Cayna had knocked some sense into her, after all. As Cayna walked toward a trash can, she let her smile widen and reveal teeth.

SEVEN

THE PRE-OLYMPICS SPECIAL went off without a hitch, despite the lack of its originally scheduled guest. The absence of Cayna was filled up with two hours of interviews with American athletes worried they were not going to have a chance to compete. It was a chaotic morning in the hallway of changing rooms, each one bursting with guests. The studio crew would get a three-day weekend after this – that had been on the calendar for weeks – but they weren't skimping on work today.

In the studio, the tense episode was observed by a concerned and sympathetic audience. The celebratory mood Ray and the crew had prepped for was overturned by an unshakably somber mood. Everyone had speculations about what had started the fire. Cayna's name barely stayed off anyone's lips. The audience —

and the athletes — seemed to be evenly split between her supporters and her accusers. Ray was starting to believe it was Cayna, too, by the time filming was over and he said goodnight to viewers at home and goodbye to the studio audience.

He thought about it in his dressing room as he took off his suit. He thought about it intermittently during lunch with the U.S. Men's and Women's soccer teams.

In the afternoon, he headed to the studio for a production meeting, and then he crashed the writers' room. The staff in general were relieved that the pre-Olympics special had gone smoothly despite the roadblocks, but their attentions were already on the next show on Monday. With the Olympics in chaos, more than half the material for next week's *The After-Hours Show* episodes was effectively obsolete. The writers were furiously writing new jokes, many of which would probably be thrown out after the weekend. But that was the business of a late-night show with topical monologues.

Ray contributed a few one-liners, and they bandied back a few other jokes and topic options, as usual.

The thought came out of nowhere and practically hit him over the head.

"Oh, my God," Ray said. "I know where Cayna Maren is. Maine. She's in Maine."

He looked around, but the group sitting around the table just looked confused.

"Why would she be there?"

He said, "Because that's where she — I gotta call someone."

Ray ran for the door and into the hall. He found the

number in his contacts and dialed.

"Buddy," said the voice on the other end. "You know I've gotta start shooting in, like, five minutes, right? Not all of us got to film their shows hours earlier than usual, like you did."

"Yeah, I know. This'll be quick. Hi, Tom."

"Hi, Ray. What's up?"

Tom Hollard, host of *The Evening Show*, had been Ray's boss once upon a time. Now, they were colleagues working for different networks. And they were constantly telling each other what the other show was up to or creating joint skits, which the publicly feuding networks allowed. Go figure.

"You've interviewed Cayna Maren as often as I have," Ray said.

"More than you, probably."

"Right. If she *did* set off the fire, what do you think her motivations would be?"

"Hell if I know. Our biggest sketch for tonight is all about her possible motivations," said Tom. "My favorite is that she wanted to make a huge pep-rally bonfire to cheer on the American teams and it just got out of hand."

"Dammit, that's one of our jokes," Ray said. "But, seriously. What if she was sending a message? Saying that she was leaving? That's why no one's seen her. It's why she hasn't been involved in the investigation into the fire. She isn't doing her job anymore."

"Yeah, it's possible. But where would she go?"

"I think I know. I've been hearing a lot of stories lately about how Cayna became the protector. Almost all of them are about how she was enticed to stay here or has a sense of patriotic duty."

"Yeah, right. Cayna's all smiles in public, but I really doubt she's a patriot."

"That's the impression I've always gotten, too, from her," Ray said. "There's this one story I've heard. I think it's the true one. If it is, I think I know where Cayna is."

"Well, tell me everything so we can take credit on our show tonight."

"No chance. Not for this. Thanks, Tom."

They said their goodbyes, and Ray walked at an almost-jog down the hall to Carry's office. She looked up as he knocked on the doorframe.

"Hey, Carry, I have an idea for a segment for the show. The catch is I need a camera crew and plane tickets to Maine for it to work."

"Why Maine? Also, where in Maine, exactly?"

"As close to Lubec as possible. It's on the border. I've been hearing a story about how Cayna was bound to the country a hundred years ago. The binding happened in Lubec. I think Cayna's gone back there to break the binding."

He explained all the details he knew about the story and why he was so certain it was the real one. He had no proof, only a hunch, but it was a strong one.

"A magic binding, huh?" Carry sounded skeptical, but she hadn't laughed him out of the office yet.

"I know, but we know dragons can do magic. Maybe humans can, too."

"Okay. But we don't have the budget for traveling, not after today's expenses. And there's no way we could do this last minute. But maybe the news crew can use the tip."

Ray bit his lip, annoyed. But she was right. "Yeah. Let's get them on the line. I'll explain everything I know to them."

The ABN News producers were happy for the tip. "It's as good a lead as anything we've got. We'll look into it. Thanks, Ray."

It was the best Ray was going to get, and it wasn't good enough. He left Carry's office feeling frustrated but already digging out his phone.

"Hello?" said the woman on the other end.

"Sabrina, this is Ray Boyer. Have you got a minute?"

"Oh, hey, Ray," said Sabrina Fetch, ABN News reporter. "Sure, we're just camping outside of MetLife for now."

"Great. Look, I need a favor." He explained everything yet again. "I need you to call your producers and convince them to let you go to Lubec. And I want to hitch a ride."

"Wow. You're that sure about this lead, huh? This would more than cover that favor I owe you."

"I know. But I've got a strong feeling about it."

"Your producers are going to let you come along? Don't you have filming to do this week?"

"Nah, after today's special, everyone's got a long weekend."

"Lucky." Sabrina was quiet for a moment. "Okay. We've pretty much covered the stadium fire from the Olympics angle, the engineering angle, and the firefighting angle. It's not like there's much to keep us in New York, not for this story. We've traveled farther than Maine when we've had less to go on. Let me do some digging into this Lubec theory, and if I find anything good, I'll go to my producers about it. You've intrigued me enough to want to go to Lubec, regardless, so I hope this pans out."

"Thank you, Sabrina. You are a goddess."

"Shut up. I'll call you back."

But she called back an hour later with bad news. "Sorry, Ray, I can't find more than rumors that this is the real deal. My team can't travel across four state lines on a rumor."

"Dammit," Ray said.

"Yeah, I know how you feel. I'm sorry, Ray."

"Yeah. Thanks, anyway, Sabrina."

It looked like that was it. There was no way Ray was going to Maine now.

And as he walked the blocks to the parking garage and headed inside to his car, what he'd almost managed to do sunk in. He'd flown across the country for the show before, but not to follow the trail of a hot news item. He was a late-night host. He didn't report the news, he just commented on it. And yet, he'd been ready to drop everything to pursue a story. It had just felt so important. It still did, but priorities kept him from going now.

He'd ask Cyndy about it when he got home and get her angle on his bout of lunacy. She was usually better at figuring out what was going on in his head than he was.

Cayna felt like she was out of time.

As the lighthouse beam passed over the area, she scanned the horizon, looking for the dark shapes of ships converging on Gulliver's Hole. She watched the woods, looking for the movement of soldiers. No one came as the moon climbed the sky. Cayna paused every ten minutes to listen and look and saw nothing but nature in any direction.

It was irritating. The anticipation made her teeth grind together. She hated having no intel. Normally, she'd be kept apprised by the military when there were threats on local soil. Now that she'd made herself the threat, she'd known she'd be in the dark, but *knowing* and *understanding* were two different things. She hated being in the dark, figuratively.

By the light of her flashlight beam, she scanned and searched every centimeter of every rock. But as the moon sunk and the sky grew lighter with the approaching dawn, she had no better luck this night than the first night.

As dawn broke, Cayna clicked off her flashlight and let out a growl. The sound rumbled out of her human-form's throat and reverberated into the woods and onto the water. The forest noises hushed. But knowing hundreds — maybe thousands — of animals were now trembling in fear didn't make Cayna feel any better. They weren't the animals she wanted to scare.

"Pack your bags and get to Newark," Sabrina said. "We're flying to Bangor, Maine, then driving the rest of the way to Lubec. We sent an intern to Lubec yesterday, just in case, and she's reporting that a bunch of armored police vehicles and cops have suddenly poured into Lubec. They're conducting interviews, saying they're looking for a woman whose description sounds an awful lot like Cayna. My team's heading there now, and I got you a spot on the flight we're taking."

"Oh, my God. Thanks."

Ray hung up the phone. He'd been right. This was it.

He ran down the hall. "Cyndy!"

Sabrina's team consisted of Ray and a lone cameraman named Chad Whittaker. Ray hadn't met him before, but they struck up an easy conversation about where in the hell the Giants might be playing home games now.

Chad was relaxed, as this was likely just another day for him.

Ray couldn't say the same. This trip was a big deal.

ABN schedulers had managed to get tickets on the same flight, but not three together. As the plane ascended to the clouds, Ray got a good look at Long Island and northeastern New Jersey. The plane rose quickly, but there was no mistaking the MetLife Stadium — or what was left of it. The plane practically flew right above the sports complex. The stadium should have looked like a gray bowl with a thick green stripe at the center. Instead, it was a blackened pile of materials, like a very expensive trash dump.

"I just got a text while everyone was disembarking," Sabrina said as the three of them headed to baggage claim. None of them had checked in bags, but the car rental service was in that direction, too. "Our intern, Hillary, is saying that the police officers are packing up and hitting the road going south out of Lubec. She followed them to a roadblock the cops have set up at the entrance to a park on the coast."

"That checks out with my theory," Ray said. "The binding happened on the coast."

Chad "tsked" in annoyance. "We'll probably get there in time to miss everything. It'll take us over two hours to drive there from here."

EIGHT

A BRANCH SNAPPED.

Something near — too near — exhaled.

Cayna was in a crouch on human legs before she was fully awake.

Major Farris had a hand up in a fist, the signal to wait. His men, creeping across weeds and between shrubs, froze and stayed perfectly still as she glared around at them all.

"Major," she said, as if this was just another day at the airfield.

"Ma'am," he said.

"I guess you're here to arrest me."

The major lowered his fist. "We were hoping it wouldn't come to that."

She wasn't surrounded. She could hear other teams closing in from different areas of the forest, almost —

but not completely — too silently for dragon ears to detect. One of the major's soldiers — a woman wearing black body armor — spoke quietly into her radio, ordering the other teams to quicken their pace.

Every soldier wore black from head to toe, including black crash helmets and black bullet-proof vests with "POLICE" written across them. The uniform was conspicuous in the green woods in the middle of the day. She greatly doubted any of them were police.

"If you figured out I was coming here," Cayna said, "you know there's only one reason why I would be here. Are those SWAT uniforms? How do you think the Canadian government will respond when they find out American military forces went on an undercover operation so close to the border?"

"For what it's worth, I didn't know about the binding until about four hours ago," said the major, ignoring her questions. He sounded regretful, but he didn't move aside, and he didn't call off his people. "But my orders are to bring you in."

"You think you can threaten me with M27s?" She smirked. "Those bullets can't get through a dragon's shield or through my hide."

"Normal bullets, no. But these aren't normal. You could say we dug them out of the ground like we were archeologists."

For a split-second, Cayna had no idea what he was talking about. But then it clicked, and she remembered their conversation about dragon-hide-penetrable weapons. The U.S. military must have found a sea dragon skeleton — dug it up, in fact, which made her think the skeleton had to be very, very old, covered by dirt and sediment. And they'd followed the foreign government's lead and found a way to break that skeleton down into bullets.

Her gaze flicked down to the chambers of the weapons pointed her way. "You're bluffing."

"You think I'd come near you with M27s if I was bluffing?" he said.

"Let's find out." She sucked in a breath, pursed her lips and blew.

A half-dozen weapons came up to bear, but no shots were fired. Instead of releasing flame, her breath emerged as mist. She blew it out in a curve. A shield of magic was one of the only spells dragons knew, but it was a very useful one. Once that side of the shield was done, still exhaling, she spun to face the soldiers closing in from two other directions. In seconds, the shield was up. The mist dissipated, but the invisible, cylinder-shaped shield was in place. It would be useful only as long as she stayed in this spot.

If they had sea dragon-bone bullets in those rifles, then the squad could take her out, shield or not. If the squad had ordinary bullets in those M27s, then the major's hesitation to fire had cost his people their only advantage in this fight.

As she turned back to face him, she could see in his face that he knew it. He'd been bluffing.

"You can't stay in this forest forever," Major Farris said. "All we have to do is wait you out."

She pulled her shirt over her head and kicked off her pants. "Really, Major? Let me offer a different option."

The airmen, to their credit, didn't back away when

she transformed, although their grips tightened on their rifles. The space inside the shield was barely wide enough for her larger form.

"Step aside." Her dragon voice reverberated against the trees, hovered just behind the airmen's shoulders, resounded from far away, and swung back around.

Major Farris didn't move. "You can't harm us. We're under your protection."

She growled. It was true. "But I can knock a tree down with my tail."

To demonstrate, she tapped her tail against a tree just inside the shield. The trunk shook, and high above, the branches rattled.

"Or with my wings."

They were folded against her back, but she stretched them both toward a couple of trees just outside her shield. If she extended her wings fully, she'd knock over those trees.

"I can't control which way the trees fall," she said.

"You wouldn't," he said.

"I don't bluff, Major. That's *your* play."

"Actually …" The major took aim at the ground near her feet. "… I don't bluff, either."

He fired. Half a dozen rounds spit out of the rifle. Elsewhere in the forest, birds squawked at the noise and took flight.

The shirt she'd dropped jumped. It settled back on the ground in shreds.

Cayna roared. She surged forward, wing extended to bowl the major over. When she hit the shield's wall, it broke like a film of bubbles.

Major Farris hit the dirt, narrowly avoiding being slammed into a tree. "Fire!"

A haze of bullets pounded against her wings and tail. Flattened bullets fell harmlessly to the ground. The airmen didn't have the special bullets.

Cayna extended her wings, and her wings collided with two trees. One broke and fell, and the airmen near it scattered. The other tree bent but stayed aloft. More bullets bounced off her, normal rounds that couldn't penetrate her hide. It would seem only the major had the means to kill or wound her.

But then a bullet grazed her left wing, shot at her from behind, not from Major Farris.

Cayna let out a pain-filled scream. She crashed down to Earth, but immediately got back up again, ignoring the pain. The flesh over her wing's humerus had a gash now. She could see her own blood.

The forest went quiet. The airmen closed in, weapons aimed at wings.

Flying wasn't an option. But Cayna had other choices. With a growl, she surged toward two of the soldiers.

The entire company fired, but this time, they missed by a mile as she shifted into the smaller form available to her. Her human arms felt blessedly free of wounds. She snatched her backpack and dashed between two airmen who were still aiming for a much taller dragon.

Cayna hissed from a flare of pain. The bullet wound had shifted to her back, right over the shoulder blade. She kept running, ignoring the sting of the air on the wound. If she could get to the coast, she had a chance of escaping and regrouping.

She could hear the soldiers on her heels, but the major called out to save their ammunition, probably because it was harder to shoot a humanoid on the move.

With that in mind, Cayna stayed in human form except for her feet, which thickened and grew scales as she darted around shrubs and branches and jumped over roots. Fallen sticks and foliage didn't present a challenge under her dragon-form feet. Finally, she burst through the edge of the forest. Her dragon feet struck the mix of lime and mulch marking the hiking path. Just ahead was a low cliff, beyond it was an outcropping of rocks, and beyond that was the water.

She didn't slow down.

This section of the outcropping was thirty feet or more wide. She knew each rock well by now, after searching through them two nights in a row. Climbing down from the cliff and onto the rocks in human form would be too perilous and slow.

As her feet left the cliff, she gripped her backpack tightly in one hand and let herself change completely. She beat the air with her wings, rising clear of the cliff, but a burst of pain from the bullet wound almost made her drop onto the rocks, anyway.

The major shouted at his men to fire. Gunshots chased her but missed as she twisted in the air, trying to make it harder to hit her as she struggled to stay in the air. She passed over the outcropping, and when water appeared directly below her, she let herself fall.

She hit the water at an angle that made pain spasm along her ribs and her injured wing scream. But the water was chilly, which soothed the pain.

The water near the shore was too shallow to submerge completely while she was in dragon form. Her back and wings were in the water, pressed against rocks hidden below the water line, but her tail and snout and stomach stuck out of the water.

Bullets peppered the water around her. More than one glanced off her belly and snout. She wondered how many sea dragon bullets they had. Surely they would have used another one by now.

She blew a spout of flame at the cliff. The airmen dove for cover as weeds and branches of trees caught fire. She blew a second torrent of flame across the rocks above the waterline. The fire burned through the algae coating the rocks. Waves lapped the fire, putting out flames one by one, but the rest burned on.

Behind the cover of fire, she shifted form to human, a form much more suited to turning in water quickly. She grabbed her backpack, which had slipped out of her talon's grip but floated nearby. The pain that surged through her as she twisted onto her stomach was almost too much. She gripped submerged rocks with human fingers and kicked against them with human feet. She pulled herself through the shallow water until she could no longer feel rocks under her questing fingers, just deeper water.

She could hear the soldiers shouting about ways to get through the flames and onto the rocks.

She sucked in a breath and dove. She swam down as far as she could in the shallow channel, which was also not as deep as she would have liked. The water was murky and full of particles of yellow-gray dirt. Fish scattered. Cayna scraped her human knee on rocks on the channel bottom. She swam as fast as her human legs could kick. She scraped against rocks again. She could only hope the rocks' rough edges didn't tear apart the backpack and its strap looped around her arm.

She was bleeding. She couldn't help that. She didn't know how visible she was in here. With luck, her blood trail would disperse in the waves. She was surprised that boats weren't in the water, ready to cut off her escape this way.

She was a sky dragon, not a sea dragon. But sky dragon wings could beat the water, to a point.

A little way off from shore, the water deepened enough that she could transform. Her good wing beat the water and pushed her through the currents. She had to use her left wing, too, to keep the course she'd decided upon. The injured wing throbbed, but it wasn't so bad in the cold water. She hoped that wasn't due to shock.

She'd go due south to get out of the channel, and she'd keep going until she hit the invisible edge of the contiguous zone. She'd know she'd reached the border when she rammed into its invisible wall. Then she'd head southwest along the American coast. There was no other direction she could go. It wouldn't take long for Major Farris to work that out. Cayna would need to make the time she had count.

NINE

THE EASTERN MAINE countryside was picturesque, remote and, above all, endless.

Ray leaned as far forward as his seatbelt would allow. "How long until we reach West Quoddy Head?"

Chad, in the front passenger seat, had Google Maps open on his phone while Sabrina drove. "Should be another couple of miles on 189 — that's what we're on now — then we turn right onto Lubec Road and stay on it for two and a half miles, then we'll be there."

As promised, they reached the turn and drove down another country road past more country homes, with water appearing beyond the houses on the left. Lubec was tiny, not the sort of place Ray could imagine Cayna Maren ever frequenting. But she must have done so, on patrol over the years. It was harder to imagine she'd visited this place before becoming the Dragon Protector.

Cayna lived so much of her life in the spotlight. Small towns just didn't play a part in that sort of lifestyle.

What had Cayna been like before she'd gained a prominent spot in the eyes of the American public? Had she liked it out here in Maine? She was a mystery he'd never figured out and he doubted he was going to figure out now. But if his wife, Cyndy, was right, then Ray's sudden interest in Cayna Maren was because the female dragon was the biggest, and perhaps the most important, mystery that had ever fallen in his lap and ever would. And Cyndy, wise woman that she was, knew that Ray was obsessed with puzzles and had reminded him of this last night.

Signs for "WEST QUODDY GIFTS" and "LIGHTHOUSE VISITOR CTR." appeared just before the road forked. Sabrina followed the signs down the road to the left. Trees became scrub, affording them a clearer view of water and the approaching, hill-topped West Quoddy Head peninsula.

Just ahead on the road, a car was parked on a stretch of grass that could barely be considered a shoulder. Within sight a quarter of a mile down the road, two police cars –and police officers – blocked the road. They watched as Sabrina brought the van to a stop behind the first car. The driver stepped out and jogged over to the van. She was a teenager — probably a college student. She came up to the driver's side, and Sabrina rolled down the window.

"Hey, Sabrina, Chad." She peered in the back seat. "Hi."

"Ray," he said.

She just nodded.

"Hi, Hillary. Get in," Sabrina said. Once Hillary had climbed into the back seat next to Ray, Sabrina asked, "So, what's been going on?"

"It's been quiet for the past hour," Hillary said. "Before that, though — there were gunshots, a burst of them like gun fire. The cops on the blockade won't say anything, but there's no way it could have been anything else."

Ray's mood instantly sobered.

Chad, who had been wrestling with his camera bag, paused and stared at her. "Tell me you got video."

Hillary smiled. "I did. You can hear the gunshots distinctively on it, too."

"Any sighting of Cayna?" Ray asked.

"Nothing the officials will confirm for me. I've been ignored ever since they found out I was from ABN News. But one of the local store owners says he saw Cayna flying overhead two nights ago, so she's definitely been here recently." She looked smug. "I got my interview with him on video, too."

"Good job. All right, let's review the footage and then speak to the cops," said Sabrina.

Underwater wasn't a fast way to travel. Her wings were designed for the sky. They didn't care for the extra work, forced to push against the current. Pain hit her anew every time she moved her left wing. The pain would be the same in human form, but she could cover more distance in dragon form.

Cayna felt uneasy and paranoid about every noise and passing boat. She was constantly on alert. There were shipwrecks buried in places that were hard to see. Her belly scraped across sharp edges of rusted hulls. It didn't hurt, but the ruins knocked her this way and that, and she constantly had to adjust her course.

She rose to the surface to take a breath, then dived back down and waited for a boat to zoom by. When the ripples of its wake had stilled somewhat, she stuck her snout out of the water and searched the nearby coast for a patch of trees. She saw houses, dived, traveled on. She lifted her snout above the waterline again and saw a patch of rocks too steep to climb while injured.

It was the wrong time of day to be stealthy. She couldn't risk being discovered. The farther she travelled, the more congested the coastline would become with human life.

Finally, exhaustion and pain wore through whatever adrenaline she had, and she knew she had to stop, no matter what waited for her outside the water. She swam closer to the surface so she could stick her snout above the waterline more often. She kept an eye on the skies for any passing planes, helicopters or parasailers.

A cityscape on the horizon gave way to a long stretch of beach with a tree line beyond it. The beach was crowded with beachgoers, but it would have to do.

Her backpack was intact. She'd lost none of her supplies, even if some of the food was now ruined and her phone was dead. In the shallows, she could see a little clearer than in the darker water farther from shore. She shifted to human form and pulled out a soaking-wet bra and a pair of underwear. It hurt like hell to put both on, but she did it, screaming through her closed mouth all the while.

The backpack began to drift away in the process. She followed it as the tide pushed it toward the shore. Her entire body ached as she surfaced and dragged herself onto the beach. The humans up and down the beach paid no attention to her, an ordinary-looking woman wearing what passed as a bikini from far away. She ignored them in return.

The sand shifted too much under each footstep. She put one foot in front of the other. The trees were little more than shrubs. She staggered into them. She kept going until all she could see was green in all directions. She collapsed onto the sand, heaving.

She had no idea how far she'd traveled underwater. She didn't care as long as no humans came looking for her here.

Her back throbbed. It had throbbed for hours already. She hissed every time she moved the arm closest to her wounded shoulder blade. Goosebumps formed on her wet skin, making her shiver. After traveling for hours in the ocean, the wound was probably infected.

Gritting her teeth, she pulled out a soaking-wet shirt, pants and her only pair of shoes and laid them out on the sand, in a patch of sun. She leaned her uninjured side against a tree trunk, breathing heavily and ready to fall asleep, even with the pain. She knocked her head against the trunk once, then twice. Mild pain blossomed on the spot, but it was enough to sharpen her thoughts, if only for a few moments.

Healing spells were not a dragon's strength. They tended to be draining, and she was drained already. But she had no other choice. She couldn't let this wound go unattended.

She had to get her arm into place over the wound. She had to twist her back to do that. The wound screamed with white-hot pain. She screamed with it and hoped no one heard. She fumbled until she felt the bullet wound under her fingers. It felt wet, perhaps with salt water, perhaps blood. She couldn't tell.

She sucked in a breath and released it, slowly. The magic flowed out of her lungs and up her parched throat, healing as it went. It crawled along her ribs to her spine. Under her fingers, the wound began to close. She hissed as the healing muscle pushed the bullet out. It fell into her hand, and she let it fall behind her onto the sand.

She sagged. Energy left her in a heady rush. Her eyes closed.

TEN

"HI, RAY," SAID Carry's voice.

"Sorry to interrupt your day off," Ray said over the phone.

She sighed. "It's no problem. I'm at the office. What's up?"

He'd been hoping she'd say that. "So. I went to Lubec."

"Uh-huh? Okay?"

"It looks an awful lot like the U.S. military fired shots at Cayna Maren."

Carry sucked in a surprised breath. "What happened?"

"We don't know much. There are bullet holes in the forest and signs of a fire. The locals got video of that and gave it to us. And we got what sounds like gunfire on video, too."

"Do you have something for the show?"

"Yeah, plenty." Ray paused. "I want to film a new cold open for tonight's pre-taped show. Addressing my trip and what happened at the MetLife Stadium."

"Okay. Sure. If you can get back here by this evening, I'll see if I can get a skeleton crew together to film it. I know a few of the guys requested some overtime."

Ray glanced over at Chad in the driver's seat. "We're heading back now."

He called Cyndy next and recapped everything for her.

"It sounds like Cayna's in trouble," Cyndy said. "I can't believe our own military would fire on her!"

"Really?" Ray asked.

"Okay, fine, it's not surprising. But it is disappointing. And makes me angry."

"Me, too." Ray thought for a moment. "No, that's not it. I'm frustrated. We just missed her! I wanted to ask her about everything."

"Yeah, it would be nice to get the whole story. You've made me really curious, too," Cyndy said, which made Ray feel better. At least he wasn't alone.

Sabrina and Chad had been invested, too, but unlike Ray, they were prepared to wait. They'd already resigned themselves to not knowing anything new until Cayna resurfaced again. Ray wasn't feeling nearly as patient.

The video made the rounds on social media through thousands of shares and retweets. It was low-quality and filmed in portrait mode, probably on a camera phone.

Wide-open water filled the background. A crowded beach filled the foreground.

"Look at that," a male voice said off-camera. "See that?"

The image shook, as if the filmmaker couldn't keep his hand steady. It zoomed in on boats off in the distance, and as the view drew closer, one boat resolved itself into a long, flat craft. Its black silhouette was considerably longer than the pleasure yachts passing slightly closer to the shore.

"That looks an awful lot like a naval aircraft carrier," said the voice. "It's been there all day, hovering on the horizon, but I think it's starting to move."

The video blurred as the filmmaker turned the camera to face him. He was an older guy in a T-shirt, sunglasses and a fishing hat. His cheeks were flushed from being in the sun. "If anyone knows why the navy would be roaming the East Coast in the middle of the summer tourist season, let me know in the comments. 'Cause I am definitely curious."

The camera was pressed to a window, looking out at a public bus sitting at a bus station, surrounded by parked buses.

"We've been stuck here for thirty-five minutes now," said a woman's voice just off-camera. "Look at this."

The image zoomed in as a police officer in uniform climbed down from the first bus.

"We're at the main bus depot in Niagara Falls," said the woman's voice. "Police have been searching every bus here. They've let each bus go after searching it. Who knows what they're looking for. We're next in line."

Another video, this one on the ABN website with pirated copies quickly appearing elsewhere, showed a smartly dressed woman with red hair trimmed short. A news reporter chased her down a busy city street, and the caption confirmed that this happened in New York City.

"Ms. Rosen, you're the last known person to speak to Cayna Maren before she disappeared," the reporter said. "Can you tell us where she's gone?"

"My answer to any question you ask me is going to be, 'No comment,' from now on," Willow called over her shoulder.

The reporter continued to film as Willow walked up to a curb and hailed an approaching taxi.

"What can you tell us about the MetLife Stadium fire?"

"No comment," Willow said.

"What about the events in Lubec, Maine?"

"No comment." Willow slammed the taxi door closed.

The stands were empty, but the camera was rolling. That was all he needed today. "Hello, folks," Ray said. "It's quiet here in the studio, but the audience will appear again in a minute. Today's show was pre-tapped. It's a great show, you'll love it. But before we get started, I have something I want to tell you about the events of this week. It has to do with the whereabouts of Cayna Maren, our Dragon Protector.

"Yesterday, what sounded a lot like an automatic rifle could be heard in a national park in Lubec, Maine," he said, "and ABN News was on the scene to report on it. Now, if you've seen the footage of that news story, you may have noticed that I was a part of the news team sent to investigate what happened there yesterday. Well, I want to tell you now about my experience there, along with the reason I was there in the first place.

"Before I tell you about Lubec, we have to go back a few weeks. You see, I discovered that no one really knows how Cayna Maren came to be the Dragon Protector of the United States of America. I've done some digging, and I've discovered that there are a hundred or more stories of how it all began.

"But one story in particular appeared more often than the others, and it was the one that I found the most alarming. Because if it's true, then it means that Cayna Maren's one-hundred-year role as Dragon Protector did not begin voluntarily. You see, according to this particular story, a magic spell bound Cayna to the United States. She protects us now because she has no choice.

"I know, I know," Ray said consolingly, imagining the protests and looks of dismay millions of people were directing toward their TVs and computer screens. "I don't want to believe it, either. But the binding is rumored to have taken place in Lubec, Maine, the very place Cayna was spotted flying to two nights ago now, and the same place where the gunfire was heard today.

"Now, folks, this is far from being the complete story. We don't know the full story, not yet. But something happened at Quoddy Head State Park this morning, and I think that Cayna was there. I think she can tell us what really happened, both yesterday and a hundred years ago. The only problem is no one seems to know where she is. She vanished the night of the MetLife Stadium fire."

Ray kept on staring straight at the lens of Camera 3. "I want to say something directly to Cayna Maren."

Her arm and back ached, sand caked her skin, and her tongue tasted salt on the roof of her mouth. But she could use both arms to support her weight without trouble. She hadn't healed the arm completely. She'd had barely enough strength to do any healing at all. But compared to the shooting pain she'd felt before she'd passed out, the lingering ache almost didn't warrant a thought. Cayna pressed her hand against the scar and felt tender, bumpy scar tissue underneath the skin. She'd have to do exercises in the coming weeks to stretch out the tissue. She probably had a scar. The scar would be a grim, but necessary, reminder of what Americans were capable of.

It was no surprise they had found a way to copy the technology. The American military liked to stay on top of weapons development. But she hadn't expected them to develop the ammunition so quickly. Weapons development usually took longer than a few weeks.

The bullet lay on the ground. She picked it up. The Americans had shaped it into a standard bullet shape, a cylinder that tapered to a point at the head. It was gray, the color of a sea dragon scale. She could see chisel marks on it, like the bullet had been formed by chipping away at a dragon scale with the help of a second dragon scale. Dragon scales from any clan could harm any dragon. Cayna had heard many stories from her clan of ancient battles where human forces had used dragons to attack the enemy's dragons. She hadn't realized how painful such an attack would be.

She was lucky to be alive. Lucky that they still wanted her alive. Lucky they hadn't shot to kill. Lucky she'd heard that branch snap when the squad was almost on top of her. By all rights, because of her own stupidity, she should have been dead. She wasn't combat-ready. The drills she'd done with the air force, navy and army hadn't prepared her for this. She should have trained more often and extensively than the occasional air drill.

This was a terrible time to come to that realization.

She didn't like luck. If she wasn't so close to human civilization here on this beach, she would have transformed back to her dragon form right there in the scrub and destroyed this patch of forest. The noise of the felled trees would have been a counterpoint to the loudest, angriest growl she knew she could muster. But she kept the growl from surfacing.

She was a fool. She had no one to blame but herself. She thought she'd known all there was to know about those damned runes. She'd thought she could just storm over to West Quoddy Head, break through the binding in the space of a night, and be gone before the military caught up with her. She'd learned nothing over the past one hundred years. She was just as naïve as she'd been the day the binding had begun. And now, she'd lost the element of surprise, and she was no better off. She needed to be smarter.

The sun was low in the sky. She'd been unconscious for an hour, at most. She needed to move. Once she found another safe place, she could stop again and work out a plan. She wouldn't stay in one location for so long a second time.

She rose to her human feet and staggered, dizzy. She needed food. She couldn't do anything else before she ate. She also needed to know what was going on in the country. She needed intel, desperately.

She got dressed. Her clothes were damp and stiff but no longer soaked. They'd dry off more as she walked. She left the underbrush and followed the road north.

The rumble of the bus, the constant jerks of motion as it accelerated for a few blocks at a time, the hiss as it hit the brakes at every red light, all contributed to setting her teeth on edge.

With her teeth bared in irritation, Cayna caught the eye of an elderly woman sitting in one of the handicap seats. The woman just looked away, not even phased. Which meant that Cayna's disguise was still working. The bus driver hadn't seemed to recognize her when she'd stepped onboard and dropped her quarters into the coin slot. The bus was nearly full, with people constantly getting on and off at every stop, and Cayna's disguise continued to work for every new person onboard the bus.

She pulled the cord when she saw the first fast-food sign on the road. She was hungry, even after eating all of her provisions not ruined by her swim.

The restaurant was packed with the dinner crowd, a noisy mix of families and couples and adults on their own. The employees at the Burger King didn't look at her with greater interest than the customers in line, and the customers sitting at tables paid more attention to their food than to their surroundings.

She paid with cash. "Sorry it's wet," she said in a contrite tone. "It's just salt water. I was just on the beach, and my beach bag got wet." That would help explain her disheveled appearance. She'd tried to straighten her clothes and hair as much as she could, but she couldn't remove the salt smell any better than she could ignore the grimy feel of the salt-stained fabrics against her skin.

The cashier made a face but took her money, anyway. "Those are nice sunglasses," she said. "Where'd you get those? I've been looking for a pair in that style."

"Pier Sunglasses," Cayna said, even though she really couldn't remember. Her human-form's shape and size never changed. Whenever she needed to update her wardrobe, she'd go to the first store she came across on her flight path, get out as soon as possible, and move on with her life.

A TV in a corner broadcasted the news. The table beside it was the only unoccupied spot in the restaurant. She sat with her back to the wall. She could read the subtitles from there.

Two bacon cheeseburgers didn't compare to a flame-broiled pig with the hooves still on, but they would have to do. Her receipt told her, finally, where she was: Seaside Park, New Jersey. She'd travelled underwater for three hours before coming ashore at the beach park directly south of this town. If she'd been flying, a three-hour flight would have taken her to California. But underwater, she'd traveled a measly four hundred or so nautical miles. She was appalled.

Then again, if Major Davis expected her to travel farther from Maine, perhaps he wouldn't think to look for her in New Jersey.

Her legs fidgeted under the plastic table. She had to fight the urge to stick out her tongue and taste the air, which, she had to admit to herself, was a strange urge to have, even for her. Dragon tongues were slightly sensitive to atmospheric changes, but they were better for sensing changes in wind patterns than detecting if a marine battalion was closing in on a fast-food restaurant.

She inhaled, and her eyes locked on the fingers of a man in a button-down uniform shirt and jeans. She homed in on the thin band of white gold on his ring finger. A whiff of solid gold stole her attention, and her gaze jumped to a woman sitting with a group of other women, who had two more gold rings and a gold necklace between them.

The restaurant was dotted with the heady scent of gold that only a dragon nose could smell.

Cayna ripped her gaze away from a dangling gold earring. The rest of the restaurant came back into focus, with its noisy human conversations and grease-drenched food. Kids were running around in the play area. Still, she could pinpoint the exactly location of every speck of gold in the building, including the gold foil hiding in the cell phones.

She'd been constantly teased with gold trinkets for a hundred years. Wedding rings, gold fillings, edible gold at the more lavish parties she'd attended on a whim – all of these things were unavoidable in human society. Normally, she could ignore it all, but not this time. Because she was on edge, dragon instincts felt safer and more trustworthy than logic – which, logically, made no sense at all.

She ate her burger. The news turned to the Olympics — and, to her delight, the fiery symbol of her resignation appeared.

She frowned at the date on the screen. If it was correct, she'd slept over twenty-four hours on that beach. A second glance at her burger receipt confirmed it. The spell had taken far more out of her than she'd realized. It was no wonder she'd been so hungry after waking.

"The future of some of the Olympic Games remains uncertain," the newscaster continued. "Olympic teams from some countries have already returned home, while others are considering departing early. Already, the past few days have become one of the costliest in the history of the Olympic Games.

"The search for Cayna Maren continues. Meanwhile, many supporters of Maren have made pleas for her to come out of hiding and let them know she is unharmed. These pleas come from fans, social-media influencers, and even late-night talk shows. During the recording of *The After-Hours Show*, host Ray Boyer shared that he believed Cayna Maren has been forced to act as Dragon Protector against her will."

Footage from the talk show appeared. "I want to say something directly to Cayna Maren," said Ray. "If you're out there, Cayna, we want to know what's going on. We want you to tell us. We want to set the record straight. And we want to help, if we can."

Cayna considered the image of Ray Boyer on the screen. That was a surprisingly passionate plea. She never would have predicted he would direct any kind of speech at her. It was equally surprising that he'd been in Lubec or that he'd discovered the truth about how she came to be Dragon Protector.

"Okay, Ray Boyer," she said quietly so her voice wouldn't carry in the restaurant. "You got it."

ELEVEN

CYNDY SAT UP in bed as the doorbell rang. Her blue hair stuck up at weird angles. Her shoulder, bare except for the spaghetti strap of the black top she'd worn to bed, showed off a tattoo of an angel wielding a shotgun. "Fuck!" she said, as eloquent as ever when her sleep was interrupted.

Ray emerged from the walk-in closet dressed in a button-down and slacks. He'd been up for half an hour and was wide awake, but he *had* to get up this early in the morning.

He frowned at the wall in the direction of the front door while Cyndy glared at it.

"Go see who the fuck that is?" Cyndy ordered as much as asked. She plopped back down in bed and closed her eyes, and within a second, she was snoring again.

Ray rolled his eyes. He loved that woman, but boy, was she grumpy in the mornings.

It was 5:45 am, the start of another work week. The sun hadn't even risen yet. Only people who had to drive through the morning commute rush into New York, like Ray, got up this early. No one who had to make house calls in New Jersey suburbs went house-calling this early.

He eyed the baseball bat propped in the corner of the room. He peered through the peephole.

A blonde woman wearing sunglasses at night was not what he'd expected to see. He peered hard at the shadows behind her, but the stupid concave spyglass wasn't particularly useful for picking out background details.

He left the chain on and kept his body behind the door when he opened it. "Uh, hi. Can I help you?" He scanned the shadows again and saw no one. The woman was alone. There wasn't even a car in the driveway.

There was something off about her smile. It looked like she was clenching her teeth. "Hello, Ray."

Ray stared. "Cayna Maren?"

"I heard you wanted to talk to me and set a few things straight," she said pleasantly. "Can I come in?"

"I … yeah. Um. Hold on." Ray closed the door. He hesitated. He opened the door again with the deadbolt chain still on. "Just one question. Last I heard, you were being fired upon with actual guns. How likely is it that you're going to be fired upon again while you're here at my house?"

Her predator's smile became an annoyed grimace. "I wasn't followed, if that's what you're implying."

He didn't budge. "I have a wife and two daughters, Cayna. I had to ask."

She took off her sunglasses and regarded him seriously. She nodded. "That's one thing I've always liked about you, Ray Boyer. It's good to be reminded that your priorities are in order. But you don't need to worry. I'm the Dragon Protector, remember? I won't hurt them. And at the first sign of trouble, I'll leave immediately. I never go back on my word."

"I don't know. It seems like you did just that when you set American property on fire."

She glared. "I never gave my word not to set fire to any *thing*. Ever. Now, you either need to let me in, or I'm leaving before one of your neighbors wonders what's going on."

Ray closed the door, released the chain and opened the door properly. "Is it true?" he blurted. "That you never agreed to be the Dragon Protector?"

She entered and scanned the living room. Ray looked around at the blankets discarded carelessly on the couch, the laptop in sleep mode on one of the easy chairs, and the coffee mug he'd left on a side table. The fireplace hadn't been lit in all the years they'd lived there. It was hidden behind Cyndy's life-size, cardboard cutout of Dean Winchester. Winchester's head was half-obscured by a fancy headdress Cyndy had made once for a Halloween party. The headdress, Ray noticed, had a cobweb.

Those were the things *Ray* took stock of – all the clutter that gave away how little Ray and Cyndy cared about keeping things absolutely neat and tidy. Ray was away from home too many hours every day to be bothered to clean when he returned, and Cyndy spent all of her time in her studio behind the house.

Cayna probably didn't care. She was probably noting the windows and doorways and all the exits and avenues of escape that didn't involve blowing a hole through the roof. At least, he *hoped* she would be that considerate if something were to happen.

"I'll answer your questions," she said, "but I want to do it on camera."

"On camera?" Ray repeated, confused. "You've come to the wrong place for that."

"Not a studio camera, a phone camera or something. Going to your studio is a bit too public. If you want answers from me, you'll have to record them now, on whatever devices you've got here. Then, you can share the recording with ABN." She smiled with all teeth. "And I hope you will, but only after I've left."

Ray nodded. "Okay. I can do that."

"Great. Although you might want to clue your family into what's going on." Cayna nodded at the hall doorway. "I can hear three distinct people waking up."

"Right, I should definitely do that." And get his phone while he was back there — and maybe Cyndy's laptop and Cyndy's phone, too. If the audio and visual was crap on one device, it would be good to have some backups. "How'd you know where I lived, anyway?"

Cayna looked surprised. "Cyndy invited me to last season's wrap party. It had your house's address on it. Didn't you know?"

He had known that. He'd never expected Cayna to show up, and she hadn't. Her aversion to human parties was no secret. He hadn't expected her to memorize the address on the invitation. Who did that?

Humans didn't usually do that, but Cayna wasn't one. The reminder was enough to make Ray uneasy as he invited her to have a seat in the living room and left her there. What on Earth was he doing, inviting a dragon into his house? Hell, what was he doing, inviting an *arsonist* of *any* species into his house?

He entered the hallway and immediately came upon Cyndy, who was busy pulling their younger daughter's door shut.

"Go back to sleep, okay? I'll tell you about it over breakfast, but you need to stay in bed for a little longer," Cyndy whispered through the door crack.

Ray caught the door and peeked through it at Rebecca, who was lying in bed and looking surly. "Goodnight, Rebecca," he said.

"Goodnight, Rebecca," Cyndy echoed and, ignoring their daughter's grumbles, pulled the door shut.

Behind them, the door to Susie's room opened. "What's going on?" she mumbled.

Susie looked as awake as her mother — both had nests for hair and, almost on cue, let out simultaneous yawns as they blinked sleepily at Ray.

"Well, don't panic." Ray turned to his wife. "But —"

The quip, "I've let an arsonist into the house," stalled on his tongue as he remembered just how good Cayna's hearing was.

"— Cayna's here," he finished lamely.

Cyndy frowned. "What?"

"Cayna?" Susie seemed to wake up pretty fast. "Oh,

my God, can I talk to her?"

Cyndy, meanwhile, hadn't experienced a burst of adrenaline. She was still half-awake. She blinked at Ray. "At 6 a.m.?"

"She wants me to interview her."

Every light in the room was on. He brought some extra lamps in from his and Cyndy's bedroom and positioned them around the couch. He had two laptops on to record sound and get different angles. His phone, which had the best resolution, had the place of honor filming Cayna's face from beside the armchair he'd decided to sit in. And Susie's phone sat on the couch to the side to pick up audio in case the other devices weren't up to the task.

Ray really hoped that was enough. He really, really wished he could call John and Aaron for advice, but Cayna was very clear about not wanting anyone to know she was here.

Cyndy helped as much as she could by tidying up the room, removing the cardboard cutout and miscellaneous other things. It was edging on 6:30 by the time everything was finally ready. Ray would have to get started, if he planned to get to work in time to get the footage to *The After-Hours* team to edit and insert in the show tonight.

Cayna seated herself on the couch with a grimace.

"Are you all right?" Ray asked.

"I'd be doing better if the military hadn't fired on me." She winced.

"Do you need anything?"

She waved him off. "It's healing on its own."

Ray realized he was gaping and closed his mouth with an audible "click." This — this was news. *Big* news. He didn't usually report the news. He'd thought his little adventure in Lubec would be the best he'd ever get.

Ray plopped down in the armchair. He turned to one of the laptops. "If you're listening, Cayna Maren just confirmed that she was fired upon by the U.S. Military. I'm Ray Boyer, and I'm sitting with Cayna Maren in New Jersey. Now, three nights ago, I made an appeal asking Cayna to explain to the American public exactly what's been going on this week. She's here to do just that." He turned to Cayna. "Cayna, welcome. Could you tell us what happened with the military? Why were they shooting at you?"

"Because I dared to do what I wanted for once. They've decided I'm a threat."

"Is this because of the fire at MetLife Stadium? Witnesses claim they saw you fleeing the fire. Could you tell us what happened there?"

Her eyes glinted dangerously. "I set the stadium on fire."

Ray felt chills at such a simple pronouncement caught on camera, but he kept his voice even. "You're saying that you deliberately used dragon flame to burn a football stadium to the ground."

"Yes. I wanted to send a message."

"What's the message?"

"That I'm resigning. I'm terminating my employment. America doesn't need a dragon protector. I will no longer fulfill the role."

"You said, 'I'm resigning,' and 'I'm terminating,' not, 'I've resigned' or 'I've terminated.'"

"That's right. I'm in the process of ... *filing*, I guess is an appropriate word ... the rest of my resignation. Technically, I'm still the Dragon Protector. But soon, I expect that will change."

"I don't think I'm following. What do you mean you're in the process of filing your resignation? Are you planning to set another building on fire?" He gestured. "Should we move this interview outside?"

"Setting another stadium — or a house — on fire is not on the table right now, don't worry."

"You couldn't have found a less dramatic way of tendering your resignation?" Ray said wryly. "You really put a crimp in the Olympics and cost a lot of taxpayer money."

"I've always cost a lot of taxpayer money. The government has paid my wages for decades. I suspect they'll be drawing money from my bank accounts to pay for a new stadium."

"Okay. But, still. There was some doubt that you were the cause behind the fire, but now that you're admitting to it, a lot of people are going to be pretty angry with you. Are you not worried that you'll run into problems now because you've got arson on your record?"

"You make a good point. Some nations, I suspect, will ban me for my actions this week, but I hope not. The fire wasn't just a message to the American people — it was a message to all countries."

"What was the message?"

"That I won't be a dragon protector for *any* nation. Never again." She turned to the phone next to him. "I mean no countries any ill will. My actions as Dragon Protector in World War II, 2001 and at other times do not reflect my personal views or desires. I was doing my duty on those occasions. But I will not do that duty anymore, not for anyone. I am a dragon. I am not here to fight human wars."

"It sounds like you're pretty unhappy being the Dragon Protector," he said. "Why do it for so long if you didn't want to do it?"

She scoffed. "Because I had no choice."

This was it. This was the moment when the truth would finally come out. Ray leaned forward. "What do you mean that you had no choice?"

"I was forced into this role. I was bound to this country, cast under a spell so that I would protect the citizens of this land and defend them against anyone who would cause them harm, in any way that the government saw fit to use me."

"But how could that even be possible? How can the United States government force a dragon to do any of that?"

"They didn't. An American citizen did." Her lips curled into a snarl. "Just a common man possessing dangerous knowledge. I made the mistake of trusting him until it was too late."

"What happened?" Ray asked.

Cayna took a moment to answer. "I think I should start further back in time. What do you know about dragons in history?"

"I know that dragons used to have regular roles in warfare," Ray said. "The Hundred Years' War, Genghis Khan's conquests, even in Roman times. Dragons transported human soldiers or helped to lay siege to cities and castles a lot."

"'Transported human soldiers.'" Ray half-expected embers to spew out with the words as she spit them out. "That's an interesting way to put it. The truth is we were mounts and siege weapons. We were seen as being beneath humans, on par with horses, despite our obvious intelligence. We were traded and bred and trained for battle. But that was centuries ago. What do you know about what happened later?"

"Dragons started rebelling and escaped to live outside of human society. And the Catholic Church began a campaign that encouraged dragon slaying in the West. The fact that they could do magic only further damned them in the church's opinion."

"Yes, that's correct," Cayna said with a growl.

"But you never had to live through most of that, right?"

"No. But my parents and grandparents did."

She treated him to a look full of anger. He didn't think it wasn't directed at him, but it was still unnerving.

"We were left to deal with the aftermath. Do you know what that was?" she asked.

"Anytime a dragon was spotted near a town, the townspeople would hunt them down. And if a dragon was found disguising themself as a member of the town, their friends and family — human or not — would often be tortured or killed alongside them."

She nodded. "Yes. That's the world I knew, as a young dragon."

He tried to picture what that world would have been

like. He knew the hunts had begun centuries before Cayna was born and had continued for a long time. Before and even during the time when Michelangelo was sculpting his masterpiece of the Red Dragon, Julius Caesar's prized dragon, real dragons were being hunted down. The extinction of dragons was one of the biggest regrets of nature conservationists and historians, but it was often viewed in the same light as the extinction of woolly mammoths: the fault of humankind, but something that happened a long time ago, when humans were ignorant of what they had done until long after it was all over. One dragon still existed, but it wasn't possible to continue a species with only one member of it. Far in the future when Cayna passed away, that would be it.

"My grandparents' generation was the last generation to be exploited in battle," Cayna said. "Did you know that? And after that, we were treated like pariahs and demons. But what happened later than that? What have historians recorded about dragons in the modern age?"

"Well, not much," Ray said. "Dragons were around continuously up until the nineteenth century, but in much lower numbers. They went extinct, except for you, in the early twentieth century."

"Hmm. I *thought* that was the common view of history."

"And what's your view?"

"When I was hatched, I was *free*," she said. "My clan had vowed never to be brutally used in human warfare and conquest ever again, and I am the only dragon to be used in such a way in centuries."

"So, you're saying being a protector for a human country is antithetical to what it means to be a dragon in the modern age?"

Ray wasn't sure he liked her glance of approval any more than any other expression on her face. "That is exactly what I'm saying. I hatched in an age when dragons were nomads. We no longer had a place in the world order, and we had to stay constantly on the move to avoid hunters. My childhood and adolescence were spent living in forests and migrating like birds."

"That doesn't sound like much fun."

"It was *my life*." She gave him another glare, this one just for him.

He put up his hands. "Sure, of course. But you were essentially in exile."

"Exile from human civilization, yes. But we weren't human. We were free to develop our own culture." She huffed. "Historians have asked me what it was like to be alive in Victorian times, during the time of wars between Americans and the First Nations, during World War I, during the Suffrage Movement —" She shrugged. "— and I have no answers they've cared to hear. I had very little knowledge of human events occurring during those decades. I learned about your species' history after becoming your country's protector."

"You said an enchantment makes you act as dragon protector. Can you explain what you mean?"

"Dragons are not the only species that possess magic, as you know. Magic is just less common among humans, especially with the rise of Christianity leading to the annihilation of so many human practitioners."

"So, a human magician cast a spell on you?"

She nodded. "In a way. You see, my nest-mates and I —"

Ray's interest was piqued at the word "nest-mate," which he'd never heard before. He took a note of it and kept on listening.

"— spent a lot of time on the coast of Maine. It was a hangout, I guess, away from our elders." She smiled like it was a good memory. "You can even find the remains of our old nest in Cutler, on display in a museum built around the nest."

"I've heard of that museum, but I didn't realize that nest was yours."

"It used to be."

"So, what happened? Why'd you stop using that nest?"

Her smile turned sour. "Well, we had several friendships with the humans living in the area. There were a few small communities in Maine and nearby in Canada. We weren't welcome in those towns, not in our dragon forms. But we would shift to our human forms and go in disguise into town, and we'd learn what the townspeople thought about the dragons they'd seen flying around the area. Some of them didn't want us there, but some people spoke in our defense. We approached our defenders and became friends with them in secret."

"Wow. That sounds really risky."

"It was. But we thought it was worth it. Our human friends would keep us apprised of anything their towns did that would affect us, but that was only part of it. We also enjoyed their companionship."

"But things went wrong?"

"Yes, when I met Edward Edmunds." She shifted in her seat, like she wanted to burst from it and maybe through the roof, too. "I thought he could be trusted, and for a while, he gave us no reason to believe otherwise. We kept our visits a secret from the other residents of Lubec. He was a fisherman and lived with his wife on the coast. His wife, Deborah, kept our secret, too, but kept her distance."

This time, he didn't imagine the smoke escaping from her mouth as well as her nose.

"Er, no torching the house, please," he said, hoping to cut the tension.

She relaxed, a smidgeon. He did, too.

"My apologies." She took a deep breath that was smoke-free. "I often wonder what changed. Maybe Deborah convinced him that we couldn't be trusted. Maybe Edward's true feelings were hidden so deep we didn't see his true intentions until he was ready to strike. But the result was that we trusted him too much. He had knowledge of a ritual used to control dragons. My kind hadn't seen it in use since dragons were used as steeds. My ancestors did their best to eradicate the knowledge. I never thought a random fisherman in Maine would know it." She sounded bitter. "I believe the ritual was passed down to him through his family, but I'll never really know. He never told us he knew the ritual. Perhaps that should be enough proof that he never trusted us like we trusted him, and he'd intended to deceive us from the start.

"I came to see him one day. It was a day like any

other. We always met near the West Quoddy Head Lighthouse, but out of sight of the lighthouse keepers. That day, I spotted him standing on an outcropping of rocks called Gulliver's Hole. As soon as I landed, I saw he'd cut himself, and blood dripped from his hand. A lot of human spells involving require runes to be drawn in blood. And he told me it was too late." Anger burned in her eyes. "The ritual bound me to the country and made me its protector. He told me I was too dangerous to allow to go free and that it was better if I was contained the only way he knew how. His conviction had seemed to come out of nowhere. I wonder now if his opinions about dragons had formed long before I'd met him, and I'd had no chance of changing his mind, even though I'd only ever been friendly to him.

"I called for help from my nest-mates, who were nearby. They came flying, but they couldn't undo the binding; none of them were strong enough, and neither was I. We were too young. They attacked Edmunds, but the binding urged me to protect him." She stared intensely at the phone's camera. "I turned on my nest-mates. They would not fight me. They fled back to our clan. I couldn't follow. The binding would not let me."

Everything she said sounded horrible. Ray asked, "What happened to Edward Edmunds?"

"He escaped. I found him. I could not harm him, no matter how much I wished to do just that."

"And what about the runes?"

Cayna growled low in her throat. "I cannot find them. I have returned to Gulliver's Hole, and the runes are not there. They have turned invisible."

"Hmm," said Cyndy.

Ray startled.

Cayna glanced inquiringly toward the doorway to the hallway, where Ray's wife leaned against the frame.

"If it were me casting that spell," she said, "I wouldn't draw the runes on a bunch of random rocks."

Cayna's eyes narrowed. "What do you mean?"

"Why that spot? Why not somewhere else? That wasn't even where he would moor his boat, is it? Did you guys even meet up there very often?"

"We did occasionally. You're right, we met at other spots far more often. But his blood was freshly drawn. The runes have to be on that spot."

"What if he was misleading you, though? I just think it's really suspicious that the runes would just be gone. The magic should have kept them permanently etched in the spot, right?"

Cayna's stare was as sharp as a blade, but Cyndy was so deep in thought she didn't seem to notice.

"So, where would you put the runes, then?" Ray asked.

"Someplace significant. Like one of those other places where you'd meet, or the docks where he'd launch his boat, or his boat. Even the lighthouse is more important."

Cayna launched herself from her chair so fast it sent Ray's heart pounding. She stalked to one end of the room, turned sharply and stalked to the opposite end. The pacing didn't set Ray at ease, especially since it seemed that she was unconsciously flexing fingers that he knew could turn into claws in a blink.

"The boat and docks wouldn't work," she said. "The

docks are too public. If the real runes were there, word would have gotten around. And the boat wouldn't work because the spot has to be stationary."

"So that leaves the lighthouse."

Cayna shook her head rapidly. "No. The lighthouse keepers would have seen it."

Ray shrugged. "Easier to bribe one or two people to stay quiet than a whole fleet of fishermen and other dock workers."

Cayna huffed. A small trail of smoke escaped from her mouth. "There are too many questions. Too many possibilities I never considered."

Cyndy held out her hand to Ray. "Have you got enough footage for the show? Hand me my laptop. I want to see what I can find out about that lighthouse."

Cayna stilled. "Whatever you find, it won't be enough. I will have to return there and see for myself."

Ray was appalled. "You can't be serious. Soldiers and cops are still over there. They'll be waiting for you."

She scowled.

"You need intel," Cyndy said with a nod. She grinned at Ray. "Where'd we put Gretta, babe?"

Cayna's head tilted, like an eagle inspecting a tasty rabbit. "Gretta?"

"It's her drone," Ray said with a theatrical sigh, even while seventy percent of him was tense and maybe a little too watchful of Cayna's body language. He did not like how motionless she'd become. "It's in the basement."

"It can travel over four miles and stay in the air for twenty-seven minutes," Cyndy said. "And it's got a camera that syncs to an app, so you can watch the feed live. It's the perfect intel-gathering device!"

Cayna's lips curled into a pleased smile. "That is a tempting offer." She finally glanced away from Cyndy, and Ray breathed a little easier. Cayna returned to pacing. "No. It wouldn't work," she said after a moment. "The only way to approach the peninsula again is by water, and I can't carry your drone underwater without ruining it."

"Underwater? Wait, how *did* you get here from Maine, anyway?" Ray asked.

"Swimming. And then by bus," Cayna said offhandedly as she paced.

"Oh." Cyndy deflated and scowled at the floor. "Yeah, that wouldn't work."

"She could borrow the car," came Susie's voice from the corridor.

"I don't think that would be a good idea —" Ray started.

"It really wouldn't," said Cyndy. "Some friends of mine were heading to Niagara Falls today but got stopped by a road block. There are road blocks all over upstate New York. No one knows why." She glanced at Cayna. "I bet the police are looking for you. So, you can't go by car."

"Yes." Cayna paused. "The closer I get to West Quoddy Head, the more resistance I'll find. It won't matter which way I go." She scowled at nothing in particular.

"Then ... what's the plan?" Cyndy said.

Cayna's sharp gaze landed on Ray, and he repressed a shudder. "Get that interview on the air, Ray. But do it on your show tonight, not sooner. I need time to get back."

"What are you going to do?" Ray asked.

"It would be better if I didn't tell you, I think. Thank you, Cyndy Boyer. Ray Boyer. Susie Boyer."

And with that, she strode past Cyndy and Susie and out the front door. It clicked shut behind her.

He went to the window and watched her walk on two legs down the street. She'd donned her hat and sunglasses. She looked like an average commuter on her way to the bus stop. In fact, she wasn't far behind a man in a suit carrying a backpack – Ray's neighbor, who always left around this time in the morning to catch the bus to the train station.

If she was going to walk back to Maine, it would take her days to get back. Ray had a feeling she'd be there sooner, though.

An insane part of him wanted to be there when she arrived at West Quoddy Head. The more rational part of him that liked safety knew how to override the crazy part. But, still, that danger-loving part of him was still there, feeling left out.

TWELVE

A DRONE WAS not something most humans possessed. Why Cyndy would own one, Cayna did not know. But she did not wonder why humans made such things in the first place. She'd never wondered about the human obsession with flight, which continued to manifest itself in more and more creative ways, drones included. Flying was, after all, one of the most amazing feats possible by dragon or other creature. Cayna was baffled only by those humans who were scared of flight or even, of all things, heights.

But a drone would do her no good today, because she couldn't take her time getting back to Maine. She'd lost the element of surprise. She'd retreated, regrouped, gathered all the intel she was likely to get. The longer she waited to return to West Quoddy Head, the stronger the opposition would be. She didn't have time to hike, to drive, to swim. Her only asset now would be speed.

Three blocks from the Boyers' home, she tipped her hat off her head and tossed it into the ditch beside the road. The businessman she'd been trailing behind turned toward the sound.

Cayna plucked her sunglasses off her nose and let them fall on the road. She tore off one shoe, then the other, before gripping the edge of her shirt and tugging it up over her head.

"Whoa!" The businessman stared as she stripped. "Lady —"

She met his wide-eyed stare.

He blanched. "You're —"

She showed him teeth as she slipped off her pants. "Want to see a magic trick?"

He turned and ran. He didn't turn back around to see her change.

Cayna rose into the air, wings spread wide and pumping as she climbed. She soared, letting the wind caress her scales for the first time in days. It felt wonderful as it pressed against her muscles, fighting against her as she flew higher and higher.

She didn't know what she'd find at the peninsula in Maine. But this was the only true way to do it, she realized: with the clouds surrounding her and a stream of smoke trailing from her snout.

The world inside the cloud was soft-gray and solid. Water brushed her scales and pressed against her snout. When she passed through the cloud, she saw a flash of blue sky. She entered the next cloud, then the next.

She dipped down until the cloud cover thinned enough that she could see the ground. She got her bearings, rose back to the middle of the cloud and continued onward. Each cloud came and went quickly, but not fast enough. She picked up speed. She dipped her head down for the twelfth time and saw the Eastern-most tip of the continental United States appear, a tiny oval among much larger splotches of land. The clouds hid her approach all the way here, but he clouds would not cover her descent to the ground. She wished she could wait for night, but time was against her now. She dived.

Tourists should have been roaming the island as usual, but a cop car, easily spotted from above, blocked the only road onto the peninsula. The rest of the park seemed unmanned. No jeeps patrolled the road or sat in the parking lots. The buildings on the north side seemed empty. She saw no military personnel anywhere.

They had to be hiding in the forest, waiting, laying a trap.

She pulled out of the dive and turned instead. She circled the air above the forest. Her wingbeats stirred up a wind that shifted the branches of every tree. She moved fast, faster than one of their planes or helicopters could have moved, until she'd whipped the entire forest into a frenzy. Branches crashed against branches. Tree trunks swayed with groans. Any men or women hiding under the canopy would have trouble sitting still as branches tumbled down on them. They couldn't possibly shoot at her through the chaos, either, although they might try.

But no one did. The police at the park entrance saw her as she circled above them. They started shouting. But the peninsula itself was so eerily quiet.

Hackles raised and on edge, she tightened her circle to the eastern end of the island, then to the picnic area around the lighthouse. The entire structure appeared empty, with the light on top inert now that day had broken. The windows of the adjacent house were dark. Still, Cayna did not like how exposed the area was in the morning light. She liked even less how *abandoned* it seemed – abandoned by groundskeepers, abandoned by visitors, abandoned by park rangers.

She didn't know what the soldiers were waiting for. But the lighthouse would become a bonfire today.

She sucked in a breath of air. Her inner furnace was ready to fire. Steam escaped her mouth. She began to exhale —

The house's door opened. A figure stepped onto the landing at the top of the wheelchair ramp. Clad in black, one hand gripping the M27 strapped to his chest, Major Farris looked up.

The binding latched on tight and turned her head to the side. The brick maintenance building near the lighthouse went up in flames as her fireball smashed through its shingled roof.

Major Farris turned his head sharply in that direction, but the brick building was out of his line of sight. Perhaps he could see the fire through the windows of the house.

Her landing was all force, fast and brutal. The picnic bench where she'd eaten lunch days ago became kindling as she crushed it underfoot. She dug her talons into the splintered wood and listened to it crunch. Her balance shifted as the wood cracked.

"Where are the runes?" Her voice reverberated in the

open clearing.

"It's more a question of where they *aren't*," the major answered. "Don't you have to break all of them? Didn't you think that, maybe, your old boyfriend would have written them over and over again on every inch of this lighthouse?"

She growled. "Then I'll turn the entire thing into a bonfire, just like I did with MetLife Stadium."

"No, I don't think so. If dragon flame was all it took, you would have set Gulliver's Hole on fire. I can't let you break the binding and get your revenge." Major Farris took a step back until he was almost flush with the door. "As long as I'm here, you're not going anywhere."

Cayna glanced up. If planes were coming, they weren't here yet. But she didn't doubt they were on their way. Her window of opportunity was closing. Major Farris was right. She didn't have time to destroy dozens, perhaps hundreds, of runes, presumably hiding underneath the paint of the lighthouse walls. But she shouldn't have to. A binding couldn't be reinforced or strengthened. Only one set of runes was necessary. Major Farris didn't know that, and apparently, neither had Edward Edmunds. Truly, Cayna wasn't sure she remembered that correctly. Perhaps the entire lighthouse structure was covered in runes, but she was mostly certain she only had to destroy one set of them. The rest wouldn't affect her at all. They would be decoys.

"You told me you don't bluff," she said, "and maybe that's true when you know what you're talking about. But you know nothing about magic. And you're a horrible bullshitter."

The air from her wingbeats flattened him against the door. He fought against the wind to bring his weapon to bear, but she was already off the ground. She rose over the house's roof and circled to the far side of the tower, putting her out of range of any gunshots.

The chamber at the top of the lighthouse was capped by a small roof. Her talons dug into the bright-red shingles. She yanked each shingle loose and flung them away across the picnic area. Some pieces flew into the burning wreckage of the maintenance building. The sight gave her satisfaction. It was only the start.

Two open-air observation decks wrapped around the lightbulb chamber. Cayna dipped down from the roof, reached out with her foreleg talons and latched onto the railing of the upper deck. She transformed as she hauled herself over the railing and landed on the deck with human feet. The chamber door was locked. She glanced at the simple lock but didn't bother with it. She let her hand shift back into a blue-scaled paw and rammed her it against the closest window. The glass smashed with one blow. She pulled out glass shards, gripped the top sides of the window and climbed on through.

Her human feet turned to dragon feet before she put her weight on the glass littering the floor. There was no air conditioning in here, only hot air that slowly escaped out the broken window. She stood there, half-human, half-dragon, and stared hard at the mechanism dominating the chamber. The bulky lens took up most of the space in the chamber, circular in shape, made up of dozens of transparent slats attached to a steel frame. Through the slats, she could see the lightbulb, a relatively tiny affair.

Runes were etched onto every slat of the lens. They were unmistakable. She scratched a claw through several of them. She ripped off several slats, tearing them free from the steel frame, and threw them at the floor near her feet. But destroying the runes did nothing, which meant they were decoys.

Cayna peered through the destroyed lens at the lightbulb. Runes had been etched into it, as well. Too small to see in the beam of light the floodlight had sent into the dark of night for a century. Only someone standing directly before the bulb could see them.

The bulb couldn't possibly be the same one from a hundred years ago. Edward Edmunds had foolishly etched the working runes onto a removable piece. As a result, they'd have to be engraved anew in each new lightbulb, which meant the knowledge had been passed down.

If she'd known, she could have gained her freedom so much sooner. She released a growl at the thought.

She reached through the hole in the lens and cupped the bulb in her scaly paws. She knew only a handful of spells. She only hoped she had chosen to try the correct one.

She thought of shifting, of changing form, something she did so often it required no effort. She thought of shifting her feet, her arms, and focused on the energy building in her muscles and bones, waiting to direct the change. But she resisted. She sent the energy outwards, instead, down into her toes and talons and out, out, into the lightbulb.

She poured all the energy she could stand into the

glass. All the energy she needed to complete a change from human form to dragon form and back again, several times over, enveloped the light bulb.

Transformation magic was not easily shared, even among senior dragons. When she was younger, her attempts had never worked. She'd stopped trying decades ago. But these past few weeks, she'd been practicing. It was a heap of magic — more than she'd channeled into any spell, far more than the spell she'd used to extract the bullet from her back.

She felt ravenous. She felt dizzy. She banged her head against the steel frame of the lens. The shock reverberated through her human-form skull, jolting her into awareness. If she survived until later, she could easily tear through a whole pack of wolves and then sleep for a solid month.

Sand poured out of her palms and rained down on the mechanism below. She pulled her arms away. The lightbulb was gone. The runes were destroyed.

A faint light flared in the corner of her vision. She looked that way and saw one of the runes on the lens glow. The binding magic was transferring to one of the decoys, activating it.

She growled in rage. She had seconds before it took effect. She opened up her human mouth and let the fire in her lungs burst forth, igniting the lens. Transformation and flame: a dragon's greatest strengths. That was what it would take to break a curse like this.

And if she was wrong, she didn't deserve to break the curse and be free.

The flames enveloped the lens. She stepped back, sucked in another breath and spread the fire across the entire chamber. Let the glass melt. Let the steel collapse. Let the entire brick tower fall.

Flames spread from the light to the ceiling above. Sparks and smoke flared from the mechanism at the base of the light. A bright flash of light drew her attention to the ceiling, where more smoke and sparks rained down on the chamber.

Bullets pounded into the glass windows of the chamber, shattering them.

Cayna ducked low, out of sight.

The tower squealed. The ceiling began to buck. The fire was searing. It was everywhere around her.

The flames lapped at her skin, threatening to burn her. Her scales could resist it; the parts of her covered in human skin were too vulnerable.

She let the change come fully and burst up, up, into the ceiling, then the roof. She tore through each layer, pounded against the next, and then she was through. Roofing materials spun through the air toward the ground and the nearby trees.

A wave of dizziness washed over her. She couldn't tell the sky from the ground. She beat her wings frantically. She had to stay aloft. She needed to orient herself.

The rattle of the major's M27 split the air. Bullets peppered her hide but bounced off. He had to have dragon bullets in there. She had to move before he could use them.

She rightened herself. She felt so weak. She felt sluggish.

Major Farris had moved away from the flaming

bonfires of the tower and the house. He knelt in the grass and aimed at her.

Cayna had no more fireballs in her. She was panting for breath. She needed to land … and what better place than where the major was right now?

Major Farris flattened against the ground as Cayna dived straight at him. She angled herself just right and knocked her wing against the back of his head. He flopped and stilled, out cold.

If the curse had still been in place, she couldn't have harmed him, not even to knock him unconscious.

She landed next to him, heaving. She peered down at him, sprawled next to her feet. He was breathing.

She could kill him. It would be oh, so easy. It could be the first death of many. There were many people in this country who deserved to die.

But she wouldn't do it. She'd passed the first fifty years of her life without killing anyone. She'd killed only under the president's discretion. No one could command her now. It wasn't time to get revenge. It was time to get out of this cursed country, once and for all. Major Farris would have to live with his choices … and his failures.

Cayna challenged the sky with a victory roar.

As the noise faded away, she heard the engines. She scanned the clouds. To the south, a formation of F-22 Raptors surged toward her.

They were too late.

Cayna took to the skies.

ACKNOWLEDGMENTS

I am indebted to my parents, Janell and Frank Ducrest, as well as to my aunt Suzanne Pease, my uncle Rod Pease, my aunt Max Ducrest, and my uncle Ted Ducrest for loving and supporting me through so much.

I am grateful to Emilia Bellone, Patricia Ann Drury, Danna Halpin and Deedy Young of the Women Writers of Lafayette, LA, and to Elora King for their helpful feedback on this very novella.

Thanks also go to my excellent developmental editor, Eugenia Lazaris.

Without you all, this novella would not have been possible.

ABOUT
THE
AUTHOR

 **DANIELLE DUCREST** is a Cajun woman with a Master of Fine Arts in Creative Writing. She has been a writer and member of staff for literary journals and arts magazines. Her art has appeared in galleries and other venues in Louisiana and Texas. She lives in Lafayette, Louisiana, with her two cats.

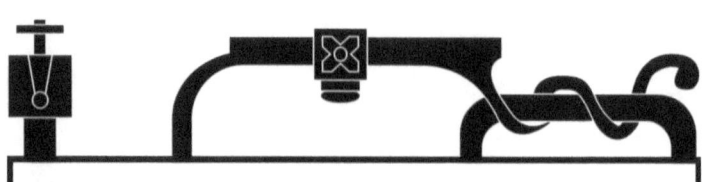

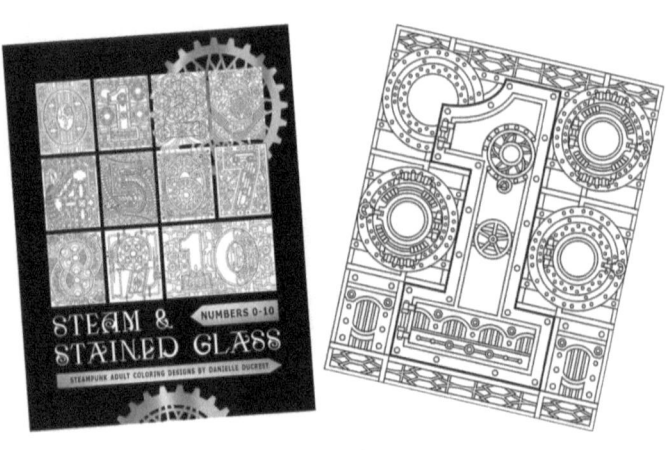

DANIELLEDUCREST.COM

Visit DanielleDucrest.com for bonus Tipping the Scales content, short stories, art and more by Danielle Ducrest.

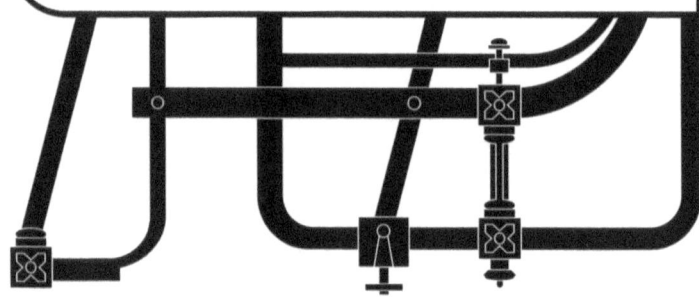

www.ingramcontent.com/pod-product-compliance
Lightning Source LLC
Chambersburg PA
CBHW050403110726
47899CB00008B/2634